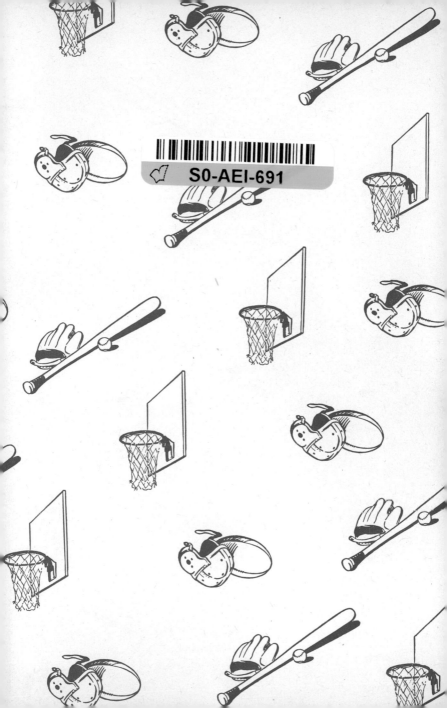

Triple-Threat Trouble

A yard from the goal line Whitty fumbled!

A CHIP HILTON SPORTS STORY

Triple-Threat Trouble

BY CLAIR BEE

GROSSET & DUNLAP   Publishers   New York

To
LOU LITTLE
Great coach, friend, gentleman,
and sportsman

Contents

CHAPTER 1

TRIPLE-THREAT STAR

THE CHAUFFEUR muttered something unintelligible to the youngster seated beside him on the front seat of the car and irritably slowed the long, black limousine to a stop. The object of the driver's impatience was a young fellow who was standing in the middle of the road holding up a hand to stop the car. He was wearing a blue sweater decorated with a big red S, and was carrying a clipboard under his arm. Behind him, the road was blocked by a white gate attached to a rustic arch on which CAMP SUNDOWN was painted in red-and-blue letters. "Sorry," he said, smiling apologetically, "I'm one of the State managers. I have to stop *everyone*."

"Mr. E. Merton Blaine's party," the chauffeur said haughtily, gesturing toward the distinguished-looking man who sat directly behind him.

The young man checked the clipboard list he was carrying and shook his head. "Mr. Blaine's name isn't here," he said, peering curiously at the towheaded boy seated beside the driver.

E. Merton Blaine's rear-seat companion quickly leaned forward. "I'm Coach Bill Carpenter," he said.

"Tech High School." He held out a sheet of paper. "This might help. It's a letter from Coach Ralston."

The manager glanced at the letter and smiled. "No doubt about that," he said. "He's the big boss around here." He nodded toward the boy in the front seat. "He looks like—"

"Chip Hilton," Blaine interrupted, removing an expensive cigar from his mouth. "Well, you're right. He looks like Hilton, walks like Hilton, talks like Hilton, and plays football like Hilton. Further, he thinks like Hilton when he's playing quarterback, running the team. Name is Skip Miller."

"He's a triple-threat star, too," Carpenter added. "Made All-State the last two years."

The manager's interest increased. "He's goin' out for the frosh team, isn't he?"

Coach Carpenter laughed. "Frosh team? Heck, no! He's got another year at Tech High School. Thank goodness! Skip playing means another state championship for me."

"He sure looks like Hilton," the manager said. "Same blond hair and gray eyes. I thought he was Chip's brother for sure when I first saw him."

"Just as big as Hilton," Carpenter said proudly. "Six-two, a hundred and eighty-five . . ."

As the car moved on, Blaine snorted and chucked his cigar out the window. "How about that!" he said disgustedly. "Checking every car! Just for a practice session. You'd think we were trying to get in to see the President of the United States."

"Ralston takes his football pretty seriously," Carpenter said.

"Small-time stuff," Blaine said shortly. "Why, Stew Peterson *invites* the public in to see his practices. The more the merrier."

"Peterson is big time, all right," Carpenter said admiringly.

"Stew Peterson and Brand University are both big time," Blaine said proudly. "Wait until Skip sees Brand's training camp. Makes this place look like a picnic park. And the campus! . . . One of the prettiest in the country."

The youngster in the front seat had been listening quietly. Now, for the first time, he joined in the conversation. "It's pretty far from home, Uncle Merton," he ventured.

"Not by plane," Blaine said quickly. "That's the way you would be traveling. You know how often I make the trip in my plane. Averages about twice a month. Shucks, another passenger back and forth wouldn't mean a thing. In fact, it would be company for Riggs. He's crazy about football."

Blaine turned to Carpenter. "Riggs is my personal pilot. You've met him."

"But I wouldn't know anyone out there," Skip persisted.

"Nonsense!" Blaine said impatiently. "Why, the whole campus would know you in a week. So far as that's concerned," he continued thoughtfully, "your father could move the whole family out there. Fixing him up with a good job in the main plant would be as easy as falling off a log."

"It's a good thing Curly Ralston can't hear you talking to Skip," Carpenter said, laughing nervously. "He thinks Skip is all set for State."

"I never told him I was going to State," Skip said quickly. "Gosh, I can't make up my mind what to do."

"There's plenty of time," Blaine said hastily. "Don't worry about it." He turned to Carpenter. "Getting back to Ralston— Why, he's a mere beginner compared to Peterson. It's all a matter of record. Nope, Stew Peterson makes Curly Ralston look like pretty small potatoes."

"Maybe so," Carpenter said in a conciliatory tone of voice, "but he's the biggest thing that has happened to State football for a long time. Last year was only his second but he won the conference title. Might do it again this year, too."

"You mean *Chip Hilton* might do it," Skip said pointedly.

"I thought it took eleven men to make a team," Blaine said, winking significantly at Carpenter.

"To make a team, yes," Skip retorted. "But it takes a Chip Hilton to make a team great. I saw every game State played last year—"

"And almost every practice session!" Carpenter interrupted. "I don't know what Skip would have done if we hadn't played our games on Fridays."

"Granted Hilton was a sensation as a sophomore," Blaine said lightly, "it doesn't mean he can repeat."

"He can repeat," Skip said stubbornly. "Why shouldn't he? Heck, he was on *everybody's* All-America team—"

"Hilton doesn't know it," Carpenter said, "but he made you the best high school quarterback in the country."

"Skip was All-State the year before," Blaine pointed out.

"Sure," Carpenter agreed, "but he picked up a lot of all-around finesse from Hilton. Getting back to this year, though, you might be right about Hilton *and* State. Ralston lost a lot of players. More than half the squad graduated."

"Doesn't mean a thing," Skip said, grinning back at the two men. "Hilton is still around."

The car moved along the tree-lined road, past a number of cottages and out into a wide, cleared field. On one side of the field there were several large one-story buildings and, below these, a slow-moving little river. On the other side of the field there were several tennis courts. In the center of the open area a football field was laid out and enclosed by a rope fence.

On the north side of the field, a number of cars were parked up against the side line, and on the south side, there was a set of low, wooden bleachers. The bleachers were partly filled with spectators and many of the cars were occupied.

"I thought we would be early," Blaine said.

"It's hard to beat the State fans," Carpenter said, grinning. "Most of them practically live down here during training camp season."

Although it was only the third of September and the sun was warm and bright, there was a hint of football weather in the faint, cool breeze which drifted gently down from the nearby mountain ridge. Blaine and his two companions walked around the field and climbed to the top row of the bleachers. Here they could get an unobstructed view of the players and soon were pointing them out to one another.

"There's Hilton!" Skip said excitedly. "On the other side of the field. That's him punting now. Boy, what a boot!"

"The other kicker is Fireball Finley, the fullback," Carpenter added. "He's almost as good as Hilton."

"He might kick as far," Skip protested, "but he doesn't boot 'em as high. *And* he hasn't got Chip's control. Chip can angle 'em out of bounds inside the ten-yard line any time. I've seen him do it more than once."

"Seems to me there's several good kickers out there," Blaine observed. "These two fellows right down here in front of us don't look too bad."

Carpenter studied the two kickers. "They're new to me," he said, shaking his head. "I never saw them before. You know them, Skip?"

Skip shook his head. "No, Coach. They must be up from the frosh team. Hey, one of those guys kicks lefty! He can boot 'em, too."

Over on the other side of the field, Fireball Finley kicked the ball and the plunk of shoe on pigskin attracted their attention. The ball took off on a long, low trajectory. "About fifty-five yards," Carpenter said. "Like a bullet."

Down below, the righty kicker took a turn and they shifted their attention to his kick. It covered about the same distance as Finley's. It was the lefty kicker's turn now, but he paused to watch Hilton on the other side of the field.

The pass shot back to the tall, slender quarterback, and he gave it all he had, his leg following through until his foot ended high above his head. The ball took off and up and out, wobbling and spinning high in the air until it reached its highest point. It seemed to hang there for a second and then darted wickedly downward, gliding and slipping deceptively from side to side. The receiver suddenly turned and ran backward but he wasn't fast enough and the ball soared far over his head.

"It's way over Speed Morris' head," Skip breathed, his voice filled with awe. "And Morris is fast—"

"A mile high, too," Carpenter added.

The lefty kicker took his turn, now. It was a good, solid boot, but it couldn't compare with Hilton's tremendous kick. "I've seen that lefty kicker somewhere," Carpenter said musingly, "but I can't place him."

He turned toward two men who were seated a few feet away. "Do you gentlemen know the names of the two kickers right down here in front of us? Where they're from?"

The nearest man grinned and elbowed his companion. "We sure do," he said eagerly. "The one kicking with his left foot is my son—Eddie Aker. The other is Jack Jacobs." He gestured with his thumb toward his seatmate. "His boy. We're all from Burton. The kids played together in high school. They're halfbacks and they both run, pass, and kick. Guess you saw for yourself how they can kick the ball. Eddie plays right halfback and runs and passes to the left. Jack plays left half and runs and passes to the right."

He took a deep breath, and before Carpenter could speak, continued hurriedly, "They're hard runners, too. *And* they can block and tackle. You just wait'll you see them peg the ball. Both of 'em can do something Hilton can't do. They can pass the ball on the dead run and knock your eye out with it every time."

Skip snorted disgustedly. "You're talking through your hat," he said, turning away.

Aker glanced sharply at the youngster and went on, "Yes, sir, they just about tore every team they met to pieces last year with the frosh team. You see the size of them? They're two of a kind. Both of them are six feet and weigh a hundred and ninety. The newspapers called 'em the touchdown twins. All they need is a little help and a couple of good plays. . . .

"I don't know what kind of a system the coach is going to use this year, now that he's got our kids. Lord knows we had enough college scouts parking on our porches the last couple of years they were in high school." Aker paused for breath and then quickly continued, "If you ask me, Ralston will be a darn fool *not* to build his offense around 'em."

Jacobs pounced on Aker's last word like a starving dog. "It makes no difference what kind of a system Ralston uses. He's still gonna have a tough time keepin' our two kids off the team, out of his startin' line-up."

Carpenter leaned close to Blaine. "Tough time keeping the two fathers from doing the coaching, too," he added softly.

Before the coach could turn back to thank the two men, Aker took off again. "Yes, sir," he said loudly, glancing around. "You put our two kids in the same backfield with Chip Hilton and give 'em some kind of a line and you'll really have something. Imagine! Three triple-threat men in the *same* backfield! On the *same* team! Mark my words—soon as Ralston wakes up and puts Eddie and Jack and Chip Hilton together, the sportswriters all over the country will start calling them the triple-threat triplets. Just like they called those Notre Dame fellers the Four Horsemen. How about that! The *triple-threat* triplets!"

CHAPTER 2

FAIR-HAIRED BOY

COACH RALSTON's whistle cut across the field and his "On the double!" brought Chip and Fireball and Brennan and Speed and the rest of the squad on the run to surround him in the center of the field. The tall, well-built man waited until the players quieted.

"All right!" he barked. "Get your helmets and hustle down to the north goal. Before we scrimmage we're going to have a couple of races. Nibs—Jim, divide 'em up—backs and ends together, guards, tackles, and centers. Rock, you come with me. We'll check the winners at the other end of the field."

Chip turned and headed for the north goal and the other backs followed his lead. Speed and Fireball sprinted up beside him and Ace Gibbons followed on their heels.

Fireball jogged against Chip. "Remember the first time we raced?" he asked, grinning.

"And how!" Chip said. "You beat me."

"It was the first and last time," Fireball said wryly. "*And* I had an assist. A jerk would-be friend of mine bumped into you *accidentally on purpose*. Remember?"

9

"I remember," Chip said, stopping at the goal line. "What about *this* time?"

Before Fireball could reply, Ace Gibbons horned in. "What is this?" he interrupted good-naturedly. "A private race? How about Speed and me?"

Lefty Aker and Jack Jacobs were close enough to hear the kidding. Now, they looked at one another in feigned surprise.

"I thought *everyone* was supposed to run," Aker said pointedly.

"Oh, no," Jacobs said sarcastically. "You heard what Gibbons said. '*This is a private race.*' You know —*varsity only.*"

"But according to Ralston *every* position is open."

"*Ralston?*" Aker repeated mockingly. "What's he got to do with it?"

"You know," Jacobs said. "He's the coach—"

Ace Gibbons had taken as much as he could stand. He squared his shoulders and moved slowly and purposefully toward the two bumptious halfbacks. "If you two guys think you're being funny—"

Ace didn't have a chance to finish the sentence. Nibs Nelson and Jim Sullivan, the assistant coaches, had reached the goal line and Nelson's "Let's go!" broke up the brewing unpleasantness.

"Backs and ends first," Nelson called out. "Up on the goal line. Keep your helmets on, now. Three-point stance. Take off on *go!*"

Chip lined up between Speed and Fireball. Gibbons was beside the big fullback and the rest of the backs and ends were strung out along the limed goal line. The coaches had given the squad wind sprints from the first day of camp but this was the first real race.

He glanced along the line trying to figure out his

personal competition. Speed, Fireball, Ace, Red Schwartz, Whittemore, and Junior Roberts were old teammates and he knew what they could do. Speed and Fireball were extremely fast, evenly matched, and capable of beating him in any race. If he got a bad start or didn't pace himself just right he was in danger of following one or both of them across the goal line.

Ace, Red, Whittemore, and Junior Roberts were four of a kind; slow on the getaway, but once they got started, equipped with plenty of strength, speed, leg drive, and heart to fight a fellow all the way. Chip had thrown passes to Chris Montague and the slender sophomore end had shown enough to convince everyone that he could run. He knew nothing about his understudy, Gary Young. But the fiery sophomore quarterback seemed fast. So far, Aker and Jacobs had spent most of their time bragging about their past accomplishments . . .

"Ready! On your mark! Get set— *Go!*"

Chip took three short digging steps and gradually lengthened his stride. He was concentrating on a straight line to the other end of the field, but he was aware that Speed and Fireball were even with him. He didn't turn his head, but out of the corners of his eyes he could see daylight behind the two sprinters, and he knew the three of them were out in front.

Across the thirty, the forty, the mid-field stripe and Speed and Fireball still kept pace. Now the forty . . .

Then Chip heard a roar from the side-line stands and his heart jumped as Aker and Jacobs shot slightly ahead ten yards to his left.

He was still a stride behind Aker and Jacobs when he crossed the thirty, and Speed and Fireball were no longer beside him. Then, for the first time, he stepped up the pace, began his sprint. There wasn't any use worrying about Aker, Jacobs, Speed, Fireball, or anyone else now. It was a matter of full steam ahead, pumping the arms and legs and putting out with the last ounce of strength.

Chip sped across the twenty, the fifteen, the ten, the five, the goal line and pulled up a few strides beyond the end zone. Then he turned to see how the others had made out. Speed, Fireball, Red Schwartz, Chris Montague, and Ace Gibbons were right behind him, sucking in great gulps of air. "Who won?" he asked.

"Fine question!" Ace gasped. "*You* did! Who did you think?"

"Beat Fireball and me by five yards," Speed managed.

"Beat *you?*"

"Sure!" Fireball said. "Speed was second, I was third, Montague was fourth, and Ace was fifth—"

"I wasn't second, Fireball," Speed remonstrated. "You and I crossed the line at the same time."

Chip glanced at Aker and Jacobs and back to his companions. Ace caught his eye and grinned. "Oh, yes," he said, nodding in the direction of Aker and Jacobs. "The touchdown twins wilted—came in behind Montague and me."

"No!"

"That's right," Speed said. "They ran sixth and seventh."

"Sure!" Ace added grimly. "Cigarettes and hundred-yard dashes don't mix."

"Hey!" Speed interrupted. "Nelson is about to start the centers and guards."

"Mike by ten yards," Ace predicted confidently.

"Uh, uh," Speed disagreed. "Soapy or Anderson."

Chip checked the runners. Mike Brennan could get downfield under punts as fast as anyone. In a game one had to knock blockers out of the way to cover punts and Mike was an expert at that. But a race was different; it was based on sheer, straightaway speed. He looked for Soapy. His best pal was nearly as fast as Speed Morris. Little Eddie Anderson could move, too. That left Bebop Leopoulos, Pat O'Malley, Ben Knight, Pete March, and a lot of others Chip didn't know much about. Soapy was his choice. . . .

Chip was right. Soapy led all the way. Anderson was second and Brennan was third. As soon as he crossed the goal line, Soapy turned and swaggered back to join Chip's group. The redhead was breathing heavily, but he had a wide grin on his face. "I'm really a scatback," he managed between gulps of air. "I oughta be carrying the ball for the team."

"Tell the coach," Red suggested.

Soapy's blue eyes widened and the grin faded from his freckled face. "You think I should?" he asked, peering at Red.

"Of course!" Speed interrupted. "Natch!"

"You know the old saying," Red added. " 'Don't hide your light under a basket.' "

Ace Gibbons winked at Chip. "Sure, Soapy. Tell him!"

"I think I will!" Soapy said, nodding his head aggressively. "Right now!"

The jovial redhead puffed out his chest for the benefit of his viewers and moved purposefully forward. Ralston turned just at that moment and Soapy slowed down, changing his quick stride to a leisurely saunter. Then he glanced at the coach and pivoted swiftly about. But not quite fast enough.

"What is it, Smith?" Ralston asked.

Soapy stopped in his tracks and then slowly turned to face the coach. "I, er, well—" The redhead scratched his helmet and shook his head helplessly. "Well, I was thinking that I, er, we were pretty fast coming down the field."

Ralston's sharp eyes shot past Soapy to the smiling group in back of the happy-go-lucky guard. He nodded his head vigorously. "It was a fast race, Smith. Fastest time I ever saw—"

Soapy turned to grin gloatingly toward his pals but the expression faded as Ralston added: "For a bunch of guards!"

Soapy joined in the laughter of his teammates just as Nelson started the tackle race at the other end of the field. Then the redhead retreated to face the bantering group.

Biggie Cohen and Joe Maxim were in the lead in the race and the big linemen matched strides for ninety yards. Then Biggie forged ahead to cross the goal line a few feet ahead of Joe. The others were bunched ten yards behind them.

"Guess the Valley Falls representatives did all right," Soapy said smugly. "Chip and Speed come in one, two. *And*—" The redhead paused and tried to pat himself on the back. "And good ole Soapy romps home in first place as usual. Ahem! Biggie duplicates the feat and Red Schwartz—"

"Heads up, now!" Ralston called, walking briskly out in front of the squad. "Not bad, not good! Now it's about time we had a little contact work. Coach Nelson has the play cards and Coach Sullivan has the defense formations. We'll huddle on every play, offense and defense, and work from the cards. I'll take the offense. Rock, you handle the defense." He paused and tossed a ball to Brennan.

"Offensive team: Hilton, Finley, Morris, and Gibbons in the backfield; Brennan at center; Smith and Anderson, guards; Cohen and Maxim, tacklers; Whittemore and Schwartz, ends.

"Defensive team: Young, Jacobs, Roberts, and Aker in the backfield; Leopoulos at center; O'Malley and Knight at the guards; Ryan and Logan, tackles; Horton and Montague at the ends.

"Rock, suppose you go over the defenses with your group. Hilton, run your team up to the fifty-yard line and back."

By the time Chip and his team were back to the goal line, Henry Rockwell had the defensive team set on the twenty-yard line. The offensive team huddled and studied the card Nibs Nelson held up behind the defensive line.

"Got it?" Chip asked. "All right. Ball on two!"

The card called for one of their old plays, a weakside cross buck. On the count of two, Mike slapped the ball back and Chip faked to Speed driving over right tackle. Pivoting, he slipped the ball to Fireball and spun out to the right as if to throw a pass. The play had been perfectly executed and Fireball smashed his way through the line and up to the thirty-yard line before he was brought down by Gary Young. Fireball ran right through Aker, brushing him aside as if he wasn't there. Only a desperate dive tackle by the little quarterback stopped the big fullback from going all the way.

The next card called for a take-off pass on the previous play. Chip took the ball from Brennan on the count of three, faked to Speed, then to Fireball, and cut out to the right behind Soapy who had pulled out of the line. Then he planted his right foot and fired a ten-yard bullet pass to Schwartz who had buttonhooked back right in front of Jacobs. Red pulled in the ball, pivoted, easily evaded Jacobs' weak attempt at a tackle, and picked up five more yards before he was brought down on the forty-five-yard line by Young.

It wasn't even a good workout for the veterans. They were too strong and experienced and had little trouble advancing the ball. After half an hour, Ralston called for one more play. "Finish it up, Nibs."

The card Nelson held up for the last play called for an end-around reverse with Whittemore carrying the ball. Chip took the ball from Brennan, faked to Speed, and rode along beside Fireball nearly to the line of scrimmage. Then, just as he was about to be tackled, he handed the ball to Schwartz and lit out for Jack Jacobs who was playing in the defensive left-halfback position.

Schwartz cut around to the left side of the line. Whittemore had delayed for a count of four before driving to the right. Red handed the ball to Whitty and the big end took off around right end. Soapy had pulled out of the line and he teamed up with Fireball in smearing the backer-up. Ace Gibbons flattened the end and only Jacobs was left to stop the big ball carrier.

Jacobs backtracked, his eyes focused on Whitty's flying legs, poising gingerly for the tackle. The delay made him an easy target and Chip took him out with a cross-body block that could be heard clear across the field. Whittemore was away, in the clear, and across the mid-field strip before Ralston's whistle called him back.

Chip had felt a glow of satisfaction as he scrambled to his feet. His had been the key block and it had been a beauty. But when Jacobs didn't get up, remained down on the ground, Chip sobered and turned to help him.

Jacobs was holding his right leg and glaring at Chip. "You clipped me!" he said angrily between moans. "Got me from behind."

"From behind?" Chip repeated. "How could I? I was right in front of you— Right in front of Whitty—"

State's veteran trainer, Murph Kelly, arrived then and tried to determine the extent of Jacobs' injury. "Stay right there, Jacobs," Kelly said. "Let me have a look-see."

But Jacobs struggled to his feet and pushed Kelly aside. Never mind," he muttered. "I'm all right. If Hilton and his pals want to play dirty football, maybe I can play the same way."

"Take it easy, Jack," Chip said gently. "It was a fair block."

Eddie Aker came running up just in time to hear Chip's remark. "Oh, sure!" he said hotly. "Anything you do is fair. You're the fair-haired boy around here. How come *you* never play defense?"

"I can play defense, Aker," Chip said calmly.

"All right, all right," Ralston called. "Break it up! Let Doc Terring have a look at Jacobs, Murph. The rest of you take five laps and hit the showers. Skull practice at eight o'clock."

CHAPTER 3

TOUCHDOWN TWINS

Skip Miller had watched every move his idol made during the scrimmage. When Chip blocked Jacobs out of the play, the young star couldn't restrain his enthusiasm. "What a block!" he cried. "Did you see that, Coach?"

Carpenter nodded. "It was a beauty all right," he said.

The fans had quieted while the trainer was talking to Jacobs out on the field and had remained in their seats. But not Mr. Jacobs and Mr. Aker. They rushed out of the bleachers before Jack could get to his feet and hurried across the field. Jacobs led the way until he reached his son. "What is it, Jack? Your knee?"

Jack Jacobs shook his head. "No, Pop. It's all right."

Mr. Jacobs put his arm around his son's shoulder. "You sure? Let me see you walk."

Jack shrugged his father's arm away and followed Murph Kelly. "I tell you I'm *all right*," he said irritably.

"That Hilton shouldn't be allowed to play football," Aker said angrily, glaring at Chip as he trotted around the field.

Coach Ralston had approached the little group unobserved. "Now, now, Mr. Aker," he chided. "It wasn't Hilton's fault."

Jacobs swung around sharply and looked at Ralston in amazement. "Wasn't Hilton's fault?" he exploded. "Well, whose fault was it?"

"It wasn't anyone's fault," Ralston said evenly. "It was just a hard block."

"Block!" Mr. Jacobs repeated incredulously. "You mean clip! A dirty, vicious clip!"

"You're dead wrong, Mr. Jacobs," Ralston said coolly. "Jack waited too long to make the tackle. Besides, he turned just as Hilton hit him. The block was a good one, perfectly legal. In fact, it was the kind of a block I'd like to see every time."

"In a scrimmage? Against a teammate?"

Ralston nodded decisively. "That's right. That's why we have scrimmages—to develop hard blocking and tackling." He started away, but after a short distance turned and retraced his steps. "By the way, gentlemen," he said levelly, "I'll have to ask you to stay off the field—"

"But my boy was hurt!"

"I'm sorry about that, Mr. Jacobs. But coming on the field is against camp rules. *No* exceptions. Our trainer and the team physician are experts when it comes to athletic injuries."

Ralston walked swiftly away leaving Jacobs and Aker staring blankly at one another. Aker recovered first. "Well, whaddaya know," he managed.

The two disgruntled men walked slowly across the field toward the cars which were parked on the side of the field. On the way, they met E. Merton Blaine and his group. "How is your boy?" Blaine asked.

"He's all right," Jacobs growled. "A good thing, too," he added belligerently. "If he was really hurt I'd yank him out of State so fast Ralston's head would swim."

"Yes, and I'd yank Eddie right along with him," Aker added. "It was a clip or I never saw one."

Skip Miller couldn't take that. "It wasn't a clip," he said quickly. "Hilton was *ahead* of the ball carrier. He couldn't have clipped on that play if he had wanted to."

Aker cast a withering glance in Skip's direction. "What do *you* know about football?" he said sarcastically.

"He knows quite a lot," Coach Carpenter drawled. "Enough to be the best high school quarterback in the state."

"What's that got to do with Hilton?" Jacobs asked.

"Nothing," Carpenter said. "But it happens that I coach football. Hilton's block was not a clip. He smacked your boy down from the front as if he were a blocking dummy."

Jacobs glared at Carpenter, his face red with anger. "Another Hilton fan," he said. "I can understand it in kids, but when a man can't see through a—a faker like him—"

"Faker is right!" Skip Miller said quickly. "Chip Hilton is the best faking quarterback in the country."

"Come on, Skip, Bill," Blaine said impatiently. "You're wasting your time."

Other State fans, walking slowly across the field to their cars, were talking about the scrimmage and the team's prospects. All seemed to agree that State had a good first team but that the reserves were unusually weak.

"He's a good coach, all right, but you can't go through a big-time schedule with an eleven-man team."

"Brown University did it."

"Sure, but that was thirty years ago."

"It was a tougher game then."

"Right! But one team can't stand up against three or four teams in the same game. Shucks, some of the teams in the conference have an offensive team, a defensive team, a kicking team, and replacements for all of them!"

"Well, all I can say is—Curly Ralston's got himself a problem."

"You mean a lot of problems."

After dinner, Coach Ralston, Rockwell, Nelson, and Sullivan gathered in the living room of the coaches' cottage. "Well," Ralston said cryptically.

"I thought maybe Jacobs and Hilton—"

"Chip is too smart for that," Nelson said quietly. "Besides, I don't think Jacobs has the guts to start a fight with anyone."

Sullivan snorted disgustedly. "Touchdown twins!"

"What are we going to do with them?" Ralston asked.

"Cut 'em from the squad," Sullivan said shortly. "They spell trouble."

"We can't do that, Jim," Ralston said. "We're too thin. We can't spare a single player."

There was a long silence and then Ralston continued, "I don't understand it. Aker and Jacobs played good football with the freshmen. What happened?"

Sullivan shifted restlessly in his chair. "They didn't have any competition for one thing," he said. "Besides, they're showboats. Front runners."

"They're more than showboats," Rockwell said slowly. "They're big and fast and they played some good offensive football with the frosh team. Personally, I think their biggest handicap is their fathers."

"There's no question about that," Ralston said, shaking his head ruefully. He spread his hands helplessly. "Well, Rock, what do you suggest?"

"String along with them, Curly. They might fool us and grow up."

"What about training rules?" Nelson demanded. "You saw them die in the race this afternoon."

"Let Murph handle it," Ralston suggested. "I'll speak to him." He glanced at his watch and rose slowly to his feet. "Well, it's time for the meeting. Let's go."

When they reached the assembly hall, Nibs Nelson and Jim Sullivan cleaned the blackboard and Henry Rockwell arranged the chairs. Curly Ralston's assistants were specialists and tops in their fields. Nelson and Sullivan were State graduates, loved their alma mater, and worked hard at their jobs. Nelson was small, quick, and impulsive. Sullivan was tall, heavy, and powerful. Both were enthusiastic, loyal, and cooperative.

Henry Rockwell was a veteran of many years of football coaching. He was compactly built, strong, quick in his movements, and his black hair and upright carriage gave him the appearance of being a much younger man. Rockwell had coached at Valley Falls High School until he had reached retirement age. Then he had accepted a position in the athletic department at State where he served as assistant football coach. Like his former high school players, Chip, Soapy, Biggie, Speed, and Red, he was starting his third year at State. He was a keen student of football and a shrewd tactician. Curly Ralston depended greatly upon his advice and judgment.

In a few minutes the players were assembled and Murph Kelly called the roll. "All present, Coach," he said.

Ralston moved to the blackboard and chalked a number of circles on its surface. "We will start using this huddle on Monday," he said, turning to face the players. "As you can see, I have placed it close to the line of scrimmage, two yards from the ball. However, we will also use it as a deep huddle, ten yards from the ball.

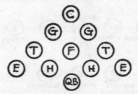

"Everyone faces away from the ball except the quarterback. The fullback kneels in the center of the huddle and everyone else places his hands on his thighs. Any questions?"

"How about the signals?" Finley asked.

"I'll get to those in a minute, Fireball. With respect to the huddle, when we're close to the line, we'll use the numbered plays and snap signals and the quarterback will call them out. Keep in mind that the close position will be used when we want to move quickly into position and get our play off before the opponents can shift their defensive positions to meet our strength. Naturally, when we are in the deep position we will use our combination code names and play numbers. Everyone get it?"

There were no further questions concerning the huddle and Ralston then spent a full hour discussing the play signals, check signals, and code names. Then he dismissed the squad.

After the players left, Rockwell, Nelson, and Sullivan moved to the front of the room and Ralston turned and placed a standard line-up formation on the blackboard. Then he sat down on the edge of the desk. "Let's talk a little about personnel and positions," he said, tossing the piece of chalk to Nelson. "Write the names on the board, Nibs—Brennan at center; Smith and Anderson, guards; Cohen and Maxim, tackles; Whittemore and Schwartz, ends.

"Backs: Hilton, Finley, Morris, and Gibbons."

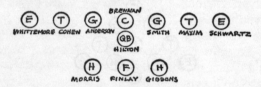

"No question about Brennan," Sullivan said, starting it off. "Mike's the best center in the conference. Six feet in height, two hundred pounds, and as hard as they come."

"How about the guards?" Ralston asked.

"Smith is all right," Nelson said. "But Anderson is too small."

Rockwell nodded agreement. "Right. We've got to find another guard somewhere. Anderson couldn't stand up under the pressure."

"No argument about the tackles," Sullivan said. "Biggie Cohen is the fastest big man I ever saw. He and Maxim are good enough for professional football right now."

Ralston smiled. "You're sold on those two fellows, aren't you? All right, Rock, what about the ends?"

Rockwell studied the names on the blackboard. "Whittemore should be due for a great year. Six-four, two ten, fast—"

"And the best pass receiver on the squad," Nelson added.

"Schwartz is a topnotch defensive player," Rockwell continued, "but I think Montague ought to be given a lot of consideration."

"He's pretty light," Nelson said. "Six-three and only a hundred and sixty pounds."

Ralston nodded agreement. "How about the backfield?"

Sullivan grinned. "You kidding? How could it be improved?"

"Got everything," Nelson said succinctly. "Hilton is an All-America quarterback. He can run, pass, kick, and is a coach on the field. Morris is as shifty a scatback as you'll ever see. Finley is a blockbusting fullback and Gibbons is a great blocker."

"Remember a year ago?" Ralston said musingly. "We broke up a senior team to break in a sophomore bunch—"

"And," Nelson interrupted, "won the conference championship."

"Right!" Sullivan agreed. "But that was *last* year. This year our seniors are gone and *they*—" He paused and tapped the table significantly. "And *they* gave us the experienced bench a championship team needs. This year—" He paused again and shrugged his shoulders expressively. "This year we've got two seniors and nine juniors left and—nothing else."

"No team can afford to lose sixteen letter men," Nelson said. "We'll be in a *real* pickle if a couple of our key men get hurt."

"We have a fine offensive team," Rockwell said, speaking thoughtfully. "Good enough to give us plenty of scoring strength—"

"But—" Ralston prompted.

"But we can't keep the ball all the time. When we lose it, we'll be in trouble."

"What do you suggest?" Ralston asked.

The veteran coach deliberated briefly. "Well," Rockwell said thoughtfully, "I think we should change our offense. Open it up. Build it around Chip."

"That's no problem," Ralston said softly. "Go on."

"And," Rockwell continued grimly, "I think we've got to shift Morris, Gibbons, Brennan, Cohen, Maxim, and Schwartz to the defensive platoon."

"I can't see that," Nelson said quickly, shaking his head. "Chip wouldn't have anyone to work with."

"Right!" Sullivan agreed. "Why kill a good offense?"

Ralston held up a hand. "Hold it, fellows. Rock has the floor." He turned back to Rockwell. "Who would you put in the backfield to replace Morris and Gibbons?"

Rockwell glanced at Jim Sullivan and smiled. "Jim's touchdown twins," he said gently. "Aker and Jacobs."

CHAPTER 4

A CRAZY FORMATION

MURPH KELLY surprised everyone Monday morning at breakfast when he announced that skull practice would be substituted for the usual group work. "Nine thirty in the lecture room," the trainer said. "Shorts and T shirts."

Chip and his Valley Falls pals—Soapy, Speed, Red, and Biggie—were sharing a table with Fireball and Whitty. When Kelly finished his announcement, Soapy pushed his plate away, leaned back in his chair, and sighed happily. "I'm beginning to love this training camp," he drawled. "Now all we need is breakfast in bed."

"It won't last," Chip warned. "Coach has something on his mind."

"He has his troubles and I have mine," Soapy said loftily.

"Sure!" Speed agreed. "We know— Food and sleep!"

"Uh, uh," Soapy said, shaking his head and pursing up his lips. "My only trouble is Mitzi."

Whitty winked at Speed. "That reminds me," he said thoughtfully, "I owe her a letter."

Soapy's blue eyes opened wide and he swung his head around in surprise. "You mean she wrote *you* a letter?"

Whitty nodded gravely. "That's right. Told me about Mr. Grayson and the guys who took over our jobs at the soda fountain this summer and—"

"She say anything about me?" Soapy interrupted.

"Nope. Not a word."

A pained expression shot across Soapy's face. "I don't understand it," he moaned.

"You shouldn't have gone to Japan," Whitty said. "You know the old saying—'Out of sight, out of mind.'"

"But I had to go with the ball club," Soapy said forlornly.

"Oh, yes," Whitty continued. "She asked about Chip. Said the stockroom was a mess and it would take him a month to straighten it out."

"You said Mitzi was dating one of those fountain guys, didn't you?" Fireball asked casually.

"Well," Whitty said hesitatingly, "that's what she said."

Soapy had been fidgeting restlessly in his chair. Now he glanced at his watch. "Oh, oh!" he said, leaping to his feet, "I gotta go!"

"Where you going?" Fireball asked. "What's the rush?"

"I, er— Well, I gotta make a telephone call to State Drug. A business call."

"Mitzi answers all Mr. Grayson's calls," Whitty suggested. "Or had you thought of that?"

"I thought of it, all right," Soapy said gravely, hurrying away from the table.

As soon as Soapy was out of hearing his pals burst

into laughter. "He thought of it!" Whitty cried. "C'mon! This is one telephone conversation I want to hear."

An hour later when the players gathered in the lecture room Soapy seated himself as far away from his pals as possible. But he couldn't avoid their amused glances. Chip was getting a big kick out of the joke. He knew Soapy through and through and the redhead wasn't kidding him. Soapy was putting on a great act for his buddies; he had known from the beginning that it was all a joke.

Ralston waited until the players quieted, and then moved to his usual position against the table. "Fellows," he said, "while you were taking it easy over the week end, we—the coaching staff—have been working." He paused to let that sink in and then went on. "A year ago, just about this time, we had a big squad with plenty of depth in every position. Still, we were faced with a difficult decision. . . ."

Ralston walked slowly around the table and then continued, "That decision called for the breaking up of an experienced offensive team, shifting the veterans to a defensive unit and replacing them with a bunch of talented sophomores—

"That gave us a fine combination. A fast, high-scoring offensive team and a hard core of defensive veterans who made up an experienced defensive platoon. It worked out fine.

"Now, a year later, we're faced with almost the same problem. This time, however, we're in a different position. We have a veteran offensive team but only a few replacements. *And*, more important, we do not have enough experienced players to form a defensive platoon."

Chip was seated between Speed and Soapy and he felt his two pals grow tense. Ralston had left a lot hanging in the air. . . .

"So," Ralston continued, "we have no alternative. We're going to split up the squad, move some of our offensive regulars to the defensive platoon. Coach Nelson has mimeographed the changes."

There was a buzz of excitement among the players but they quieted when Ralston held up his hand for silence. "That isn't all," he said. "We're discarding last year's offense for a new one. *And* we're adopting a new defensive system."

That statement brought a murmur of surprise, but, the players quieted as the tall, determined coach resumed. "Since we have such a small squad, every player here must master both the offense and the defense. We'll go over the defense later. You're excused for the rest of the morning. Study the formations and plays and we'll try to clear up any questions you may have this afternoon."

Chip and his Valley Falls pals, along with Fireball Finley and Whitty Whittemore, had managed to get a cabin together. Now, they walked slowly in that direction, each member of the group engrossed in the paper he carried.

"Offensive team," Soapy said, reading the names. "Leopoulos, center; O'Malley and Smith, guards; Ryan and Logan, tackles; Whittemore and Montague, ends. Backfield: Hilton, Finley, Aker, and Jac—" He stopped dead in his tracks. "*Aker* and *Jacobs!*"

"No!" Finley exploded. "You mean Chip and I are gonna have to put up with those jerks!"

"That's what it says," Whittemore said grimly.

"Not for me!" Fireball said hotly. "As of right now I'm a candidate for the defensive platoon!"

"Who's gonna do the blocking?" Red asked.

"I know who's gonna do the talking," Soapy said. "Chip and Fireball will have to wear ear muffs in the huddle."

"It won't be that bad," Chip protested.

"Oh, no!" Speed said. "Wait and see."

They had reached the cabin now, and Chip changed the subject. "How do you like the new formation?" he asked, spreading the paper out on the table.

"It's sure different," Fireball said. "They've sure opened it up."

"Opened it up is right," Chip murmured.

"Mixed it up is more like it," Soapy grumbled. "You ever see such a crazy mixed-up formation?"

"It's not crazy, Soapy," Chip said. "Oklahoma uses it and they do all right on the offense."

"The left halfback is playing right end when the line is unbalanced to the right," Speed observed. "What's the idea of that?"

"It sets him up for passes, I guess," Chip ventured.

"Gives the end a better blocking position," Red said.

"The fullback is two yards behind the line and the halfback is back five yards," Fireball said thoughtfully. "That means the quarterback has to do some fast ball handling on the dive plays."

"No pain there," Whitty said. "Chip will take care of that."

"He'll have to take care of more than the dive plays," Biggie said. "The entire offense is built around the quarterback. He can use the quarterback sneak, feed the fullback or the halfback on the dive plays, or fake to them and keep the ball."

"That means Chip will be running the ball a lot," Speed added.

Fireball nodded. "And doing a lot of passing," he added.

"I like it," Whittemore said.

"How about you, Chip?" Biggie asked.

"I don't know," Chip said thoughtfully, checking the spacing of the linemen. "It's sure to spread the defense."

"It looks to me as if it's more for running than passing," Fireball said. "The coach said the fullback and the halfback drive for the line as soon as the ball is passed."

"That ought to help the passing attack," Chip said. "The fact that the fullback and the halfback drive for the line means that the defensive line will be concentrating on them instead of the passer. Besides, the pass receivers are spread clear across the field. Look at this—"

Turning the paper, Chip quickly sketched several passing alleys for the receivers.

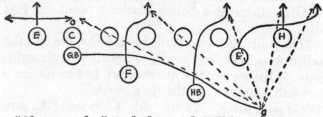

"Chip is right," Red observed. "I'll bet Ralston has all kinds of pass patterns worked out."

"He didn't give you many plays," Fireball said, checking his papers.

"That's what gives the formation strength," Speed concluded.

Chip and his pals spent the rest of the morning studying the new formation and plays. And that afternoon when they reported for practice they knew the formation and its potential from A to Z.

"All right," Ralston called, right after the limbering-up drill, "offensive platoon over here. Defensive platoon report to Coach Rockwell. Let's go, Hilton. On the ball, Leopoulos."

Nibs Nelson had the play cards and Chip studied the first one while he waited for his offensive teammates to form behind the ball. Then he faced the huddle, noting that only Whitty, Soapy, and Fireball remained from the offensive team which had upset A. & M. for the conference championship the previous year.

Two hours later Chip sighed in relief when Ralston blasted his whistle and called it a day. He and Fireball waited for Soapy and Whitty and the four of them took their laps together. Biggie, Speed, and Red cut across the field and joined them.

"How did it go?" Speed asked curiously.

"All right," Chip said lightly.

Soapy laughed derisively. "Hah! That's a laugh! If you can call bumping heads, running through the wrong holes, complaining about the way Chip handled the ball and—"

"And trying to run the team," Fireball growled. "I've met a lot of fakers in my time but those two birds win *all* the marbles. Every time Aker and Jacobs made a mistake they had an alibi."

"And *talk!*" Whittemore added. "Chip couldn't get a word in edgewise in the huddle."

"We'll see who does the talking Wednesday afternoon," Biggie said ominously.

Wednesday, after the short morning practice, Chip and Soapy took a long, leisurely hike, gradually working the tightness and soreness out of their muscles. As soon as they were out of hearing Soapy brought up the subject which was uppermost in their thoughts. "Well," he said, "it won't be long now. How do you think the new offense will go?"

"The offense is all right," Chip said, "but—"

"But you don't think we can do much against Biggie and Maxim and Red and the rest of them. Right?"

"That's right," Chip said grimly. "There's something missing."

"What?"

"Cohesion, spirit, harmony— A lot of things."

Soapy shook his head disapprovingly. "You ought to tell those two guys where to get off," he said bitterly.

"They aren't my responsibility, Soapy."

"But they keep riding you, saying nasty things, making dirty digs. *I* wouldn't take it."

"I'm not interested in what they say."

"I'm surprised Ralston or Nelson can't see through them—"

"Coach knows what he's doing, Soapy."

"He's sure keeping everyone else in the dark."

"What do you mean?"

"I mean keeping those two guys on the offensive team. Why? What for?"

"Maybe we will find out this afternoon."

Soapy grunted. "Huh! They haven't shown a thing."

"Maybe they're not practice players."

"They're not players. Period!"

CHAPTER 5

QUITE A BACKFIELD

GEE-GEE GRAY shuffled several papers in his hands and grinned across the table at Chip and Skip Miller. The only sound in the room was the soft purr of the sound recorder as it warmed up.

Chip glanced at the young high school star, noting the blond hair, gray eyes, and determined chin. Now that he had a chance to study the youngster he had to admit that there was a strong resemblance. It gave him a strange feeling and for a second he thought of his mother and wished she could see Skip Miller. He must have looked like Skip three years ago when he was a senior in high school. . . . Then, Gee-Gee Gray's voice cut through his musing.

"Good evening, sports fans. This is Gee-Gee Gray bringing you a special broadcast from Camp Sundown—State's football training camp. This morning I had a long talk with Coach Curly Ralston about some of his players and about State's prospects for the coming season. . . .

"Right now, I want you to meet two great quarterbacks—" Gray winked at his two guests and continued, "Sitting in front of me here at Camp Sundown I have State's All-America field general—Chip Hilton. And right beside him—Tech High's All-State quarter-back.

"So far as appearances go, these two great athletes could very well be brothers. Both have blond hair and light complexions and they stand six-two and tip the scales at one hundred and eighty-five pounds.

"Now—first—Chip Hilton! Chip, this is the first time we have had a chance to talk to you about foot-ball since you were selected for the All-America team. Tell me—tell the sports fans—how you felt when the Associated Press—the United Press—the National Collegiate Football Coaches Association and about every sportswriter in the country named you to their teams."

Chip glanced ruefully at Skip and shook his head resignedly. "Well, Mr. Gray, I was surprised and very happy. I didn't expect it and I don't think I deserved it, since there is so much I have to learn about the game. I hope I can play well this season and try to deserve the honor."

"You're being a little too modest, Chip Hilton, but we'll let you get away with it. Now, what about this year's State team— How does it compare with last year's championship outfit?"

"It's pretty early to say, Mr. Gray. We have a lot of new fellows out for the team, but we lost a lot of let-ter men from last year's team. Besides, we haven't had a good scrimmage game yet—"

"You've got a squad scrimmage this afternoon and a practice game with Wesleyan on Saturday, haven't you?"

"Yes, sir. That ought to give us a pretty good idea."

Gray laughed. "Thank you, Chip Hilton. It was a great pleasure and an honor to have you on this program. Fans—it looks as if Curly Ralston is going to have himself quite a backfield with an All-America at quarterback, a set of touchdown twins in the halfback slots, and a veteran fullback to round it out."

Gray grinned across the table at Skip Miller. "Now, fans, I want you to meet our own home-grown, home-town star—the great football player who gave Tech High a state championship and won All-State honors for himself—

"Skip—Skip Miller—this is *your* first appearance on our program since last fall, isn't it?"

Skip nodded nervously. "Yes, sir. Yes, sir, it is."

"Now, Skip—why do your teammates call you Skip *Hilton*—and how do you feel about it?"

Skip glanced at Chip and smiled. "I like it," he said firmly. "I try to play just like he does. Not that I can ever do it," he added quickly.

"Coach Carpenter tells me you have patterned your style of play after Chip Hilton. What does he mean by that?"

"Well, sir, Coach Carpenter used the T formation last year—just like State—and I watched Chip in the practices and in the games and I tried to—well, tried to imitate him." Skip paused and then continued hastily, "Not that I can come close but—well—I try."

"You must think a lot of the way Chip Hilton plays football?"

Skip nodded his head vigorously. "I sure do. He's the greatest!"

Gray smiled warmly. "You're a great quarterback, too, Skip Miller. And you're on the right track. You just keep right on imitating Chip Hilton.

"Now, one last question—and you don't have to answer unless you want to—I know there have been a lot of college scouts after you and a lot of University and State fans are wondering—me, too—where you plan to matriculate next year."

Skip hesitated, and it seemed to Chip that he glanced at him for help. Then the boy shook his head uncertainly and chose his words carefully. "I don't know, Mr. Gray. I can't make up my mind between State and Brand University. My uncle—"

"I know, Skip," Gray interrupted. "Your uncle is an alumnus of Brand University and wants you to play for his alma mater. That's understandable. However, I'm sure all the State fans join me in hoping you stay right here in University. . . ."

The sportscaster gestured toward the door. "Thanks, Skip. We'll be watching you on the gridiron this fall. Good luck to both of you great quarterbacks."

Gray continued on with his recorded broadcast and Chip and Skip tiptoed out of the room. The sitting room was empty and the two boys walked on out of the cabin. "Everyone is at lunch, Skip," Chip said. "I never eat lunch before a hard scrimmage or a game."

Skip shrugged his shoulders. "That's all right, Chip. We ate on the way down. Anyway, I'm not hungry." He hesitated a second and then continued, "Er, I'd like to talk football with you if you have time. I need some advice."

Chip laughed. "I have lots of time, Skip. But I don't know about the advice part. What's on your mind?"

"It's about college. You heard what I said to Gee-Gee Gray about State and Brand?"

"Sure, Skip. Where do you *want* to go?"

"I'd like to go to State."

"Why don't you?"

"It's a little hard to explain. Uncle Merton is worth

a lot of money and he's president of his own company and Dad works for him—" Skip spread his hands helplessly. "Besides, he's been awfully good to me."

"How about your father and mother? How do they feel?"

"That's the trouble. Dad works for Uncle Merton and he and mother don't want to—well, go against him."

"Why is your uncle so set on Brand?"

"Well, for one thing, he and the coach are friends. Besides, Uncle Merton is chairman of the Brand Athletic Committee."

Chip nodded thoughtfully. "That *does* make it tough."

"You can say that again," Skip said. "I, er—I don't exactly know how to put it into words, but my dad hasn't been too successful. He doesn't have a college education or a trade and he's not young. If Uncle Merton got sore and Dad lost his job— Well, there isn't much work in University and, gosh, we don't even own a house."

"Your uncle surely wouldn't be that unreasonable."

"He's got a pretty mean temper when someone crosses him and my folks are dead set on me going to college."

"You wouldn't be any expense to your folks at State," Chip said. "You could work your way. I do! Why, I'll bet anything my boss would give you a job."

"Where do you work, Chip?"

"You know State Drug, don't you? Main and Tenth?"

"Sure! I've seen Smith and Finley and Whittemore behind the fountain but I never saw you."

"That's because I work in the stockroom."

They had reached Chip's cabin, now, and the two

boys sat down on the bench on the porch. Skip had been absorbed in thought. He cleared his throat nervously. "You really think your boss would give me a job?" he asked.

"I can ask him, Skip. You're sure you want a job?"

"Am I? Just try me! I'll do anything!"

The conversation was interrupted by the emergence of the players from the dining room. "I'll see you again this Saturday," Skip said. "That is, if it's all right—"

"I'll be glad to see you any time, Skip. You're staying for the squad scrimmage, aren't you?"

"I wouldn't miss it!" Skip said, grinning back over his shoulder.

Before Chip's pals reached their cottage, Murph Kelly blasted his whistle. "All right! all right!" he yelled, his voice carrying clearly to all parts of the small clearing. "Everyone hit the sack and no gabbing. And I mean *now!* Taping at two thirty! Practice at three!"

Chip crawled thankfully into his bunk for the siesta. He wanted all the rest he could get before the scrimmage game. It seemed only a few minutes later when Kelly's siren sounded. Chip dressed in the cabin, taping his ankles carefully, and then went out on the field with his pals.

"Look at the crowd," Soapy gasped.

Chip led the squad through the warm-up exercises, and then Coach Ralston named the offensive and defensive teams. "No punches pulled this afternoon," he said crisply. "Offensive team take the ball on the twenty. Defensive team take it away from them! Let's go!"

Chip dropped twelve yards back of the ball and looked at the defensive formation. It gave him a strange feeling to see Biggie, Maxim, Brennan, Gibbons, Schwartz, and Morris facing him on the other side of the ball.

"All right, gang," he said. "They're using a 5–4–2 defense, practically a nine-man line. A pipe for passes, but we'll run a few times. Heads up, now! Right formation! Fifty-five on three! That's you, Aker, straight ahead. Right after I fake to Fireball you'll get the ball. Got it?"

"I know the plays," Aker said sharply. "You call 'em. That's all you've got to do."

Chip called "Hip!" and the team dashed up to the line of scrimmage. Leopoulos plunked the ball back on the "three" count and Chip faked to Fireball. But Aker was slow getting started and he had to wait for the surly halfback. He slipped the ball under Aker's arms and continued on out and back as if to make a pass.

Aker didn't even get to the line of scrimmage. Cohen smashed through the line, met the sophomore head on, lifted him off the ground, and smacked him down on his back five yards behind the line.

Biggie got to his feet and reached down and picked Aker up as if he were a baby. "Sorry, chum," he drawled. "Just part of the game."

"Nobody blocked you!" Aker snarled. "No wonder you got through."

"You're right," Biggie said blandly. "Come back and see me again sometime."

Grumbling and griping, Aker limped back to the huddle. "C'mon, Logan, Montague," he said angrily. "What's the idea?"

"Cut out the talk!" Chip said sharply. "Quarterback runs the huddle."

"He's right, Lefty," Jacobs said, shaking a finger at

his buddy. "When the great Hilton talks no one, but no one, is supposed to even breathe."

"Formation left," Chip said coolly. "Thirty-six on two!"

"Don't tell me, now!" Jacobs said nastily. "That means I hit straight ahead on the count of two—right?"

No one answered and Chip's "Hip!" sent the team out of the huddle and up to the line. "One, two, three, four—" Chip faked to Fireball and handed the ball to Jacobs. This time, Joe Maxim drove through the line. But he didn't tackle Jacobs; he simply lifted his powerful forearms and snapped the fellow's head back. Jack stopped right there, just as if he had run into a clothesline. Neck high! And—he fumbled the ball!

"My, my!" Mike Brennan said, falling on the ball. "What have we here?"

"All right!" Ralston called. "Offensive team again. Some offense! Two plays and we lose a yard on one and the ball on the other." He turned to nod toward the defensive team. "Nice going, Cohen, Maxim, Brennan. Pour it on 'em!"

Back in the huddle, Jacobs was complaining bitterly. "What kind of football is this? That Maxim didn't even try to tackle me. He hit me with his fists."

"Quiet!" Chip barked. "Formation left! Twenty-two on one! Hip!"

Chip made his count and Fireball smashed through O'Malley and Roberts for seven yards. Back in the huddle, Chip thumped Fireball on the back. "Nice goin', Fireball. That set them back on their heels!"

"Cut out the bouquets and call the plays!" Aker growled.

"Now, now, Lefty," Jacobs said. "Remember—quarterback runs the huddle."

"Formation right," Chip said, ignoring the remarks. "Nineteen on three. Hip!"

This time, Chip faked to Fireball, then to Aker, and kept the ball. The "keeper" was one of his favorite plays, but it required particularly good faking on the part of the halfback. Fireball faked beautifully, slipping his arms over the ball and driving for all he was worth. But Aker barely went through the motions and Red and Biggie nailed Chip at the line of scrimmage.

"Surprise, surprise," Jacobs said, when they were back in the huddle. "You see that, Lefty? Hilton musta forgot to tell his pals he was coming."

"They knew I was coming," Chip said evenly. "*You* told them, Lefty."

"Me?"

"Yes, *you!* You didn't even half-fake to have the ball. None of our plays are going to be any good if we don't work together."

"How come you didn't say anything when they stopped Lefty and me?" Jacobs asked.

"That's right!" Aker added. "They stop *you*, and *you* start crying."

"Crying!" Soapy repeated, pushing roughly through the huddle. "That's all you two guys have been doing—crying and bragging and bluffing—"

"What's going on here?" Ralston demanded.

CHAPTER 6

HUDDLE LAWYERS

COACH RALSTON's face was flushed and his voice was sharp and bitter. He walked into the middle of the huddle, hands clenched, jaw set, eyes snapping. "I asked what was going on here," he repeated. There was no reply and he glared around the circle of faces. On the other side of the ball, the defensive players remained quietly in place, absorbed in Ralston's words.

"All right! Then I'll tell *you* what was going on! For one thing, we had three quarterbacks trying to run a team that doesn't know its plays. For another thing, the huddle sounded like a bunch of gossiping old maids at a tea party. And we had a couple of would-be ball carriers crying because they got clobbered when they carried the ball.

"Now you listen to me! All of you!" He turned to face the defensive platoon and pointed his finger at them. "And this includes you!"

He paused and there was a dead silence. Then he motioned for the defensive players to come forward. When they had circled him he continued, "I don't like to take scrimmage time for a lecture but this has gone far enough."

Ralston stopped and glared at Junior Roberts who had dropped to one knee. "And *you!*" he barked. "*You* get up on your feet! When you play for State, for me, you're always on your feet unless you're hurt! You get that?"

Roberts scrambled hastily to his feet, his face almost as red as that of the coach. "Yes, sir!" he gasped. "Yes, *sir!*"

"All right! For the last time! The offensive quarterback runs the offensive team. The defensive quarterback runs the defensive team. *Is that clear?* No ifs or ands or buts! In the offensive huddle I want absolute silence. Why? Well, I suppose I'll have to tell some of you *huddle lawyers* why. . . .

"In the first place, the quarterback is the most vital player on the team. *He* runs the show! It's up to him to call the right play, to decide when to gamble and when to play safe; he is expected to spot the opponents' weaknesses and exploit them; he has to memorize a hundred plays and be able to call the right play for the right situation. And he has to know his own plays as well as those of *every other player on the team.* . . .

"When it comes to making a decision, running the ball, passing, or kicking, the quarterback is on his own —no question or suggestion from anyone! The success of the running attack rests not only upon his ability to call the right play but upon his cleverness in concealing the intent by clever faking and maneuvering."

Ralston paused and scanned the circle of faces. Not a player moved. When the tall mentor continued, his voice had lost much of its edge but it was obvious that he was still upset.

"Now, all of the planning and faking and maneuvering by the quarterback is useless unless he gets the cooperation of *every* player on the team. When the quarterback fakes to give the ball to a back—that back must run just as hard as if he actually had the ball. A fake is not a fake unless it looks like the real thing—looks so real that it fools the opponents, the officials, the coaches, and the spectators.

"Chip Hilton is an expert at handling the ball. I often stand behind the defensive team just to see if I can follow the ball and spot the actual carrier. He

Coach Ralston's face was flushed

fools me consistently, time after time—often when I know the play.

"That isn't all. The quarterback in our style of play has to make ninety per cent of the passes. He has to make them on the run, standing still, or off balance. And he has to get the ball away with five or six opponents chasing him or hanging on his neck. He's not expected to eat the ball, either. . . . That means he's not supposed to hold on to the ball and get thrown for a big loss.

"Now one last thing. We spend countless hours with the quarterbacks in private skull sessions. Hours of tedious study and discussion in which game situa-

and his voice was sharp and bitter

tions and problems are reviewed time after time. It should be obvious that the quarterback needs—must have—quiet in the huddle. He must not be disturbed by senseless bickering or suggestions. *Especially* in the huddle. All right! Let's try it again."

Chip called the play and the team ran up to the line, conscious that Ralston's eyes were on every move. Chip took the ball from Leopoulos and faked it to Fireball. Then he continued to the left along the line and faked to Jacobs. Holding the ball on his hip he cut around and picked up six yards.

Ralston waited until the players sprinted to their huddle positions. "Same shift," he said briskly. "A buttonhook pass to Whittemore. Ball on three!"

"Let's go!" Fireball barked.

"We'll kill 'em!" Soapy yelped. "C'mon, you guys! Run over 'em!"

There was real snap in the execution of the play. It started off like a repeat of the keeper, but after faking to Fireball and Jacobs, Chip cut back and dug his right foot into the turf. Aker, playing the offensive left-end position on the shift to the left, broke straight down, and then cut toward the center of the field. Whittemore, playing a yard behind the line, followed Aker for ten yards and then buttonhooked back and Chip fired the ball into the big fellow's belly on the mid-field stripe. Whitty pivoted and made three more yards before Morris dropped him on the forty-seven-yard line.

"Nice pitching!" Whitty chirped, plunking the ball down and hustling back to the huddle.

Ralston had followed the play and was waiting once more when the huddle formed. "Double reverse!" he said sharply. "Formation right. Hilton fakes to Finley and Aker and gives the ball to Montague.

Montague runs left and hands the ball to Whittemore for the second part of the reverse around right
end. Got it?"

There was no reply and Chip's "Hip!" sent them
out of the huddle and up to the line in a spirited rush.
On the "three" count, Leopoulos passed the ball and
Chip faked to Fireball, to Aker, and then slipped the
ball to Montague. Continuing his fake, Chip cut off
tackle and headed for Speed Morris who was playing
defensive left halfback.

He had no chance to see the play develop, but he
knew something had gone wrong when Speed backed
away from his block and fended him off with his
hands. He turned on the whistle and saw Biggie and
Roberts lifting Whitty to his feet. The big end had
been thrown for a five-yard loss. Chip hurried back to
the huddle. "What happened?" he asked.

"Cohen happened!" Whittemore rasped. "No one
touched him!"

"Simmer down, Whittemore," Ralston said coolly.
He turned to Nelson. "Let me have the play, Nibs."

Nelson handed the big play card to Ralston and
the red-thatched mentor laid it on the grass and knelt
down in front of it to explain the play. "There are four
key blocks," he said, pointing to the card. "I'll explain them.

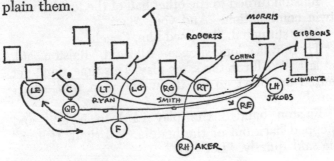

"The number one block is against the tackle—Cohen!" Ralston quickly wrote Cohen's name above the defensive left tackle.

"That was Jacobs' responsibility," he said, writing Jacobs' name on the card. Ralston wrote Schwartz's name below the defensive left-end position. "Smith did a good job on Schwartz.

"The third block was a delayed block by Ryan on Gibbons. Ryan's timing and his block were perfect."

Ralston paused and glanced at Aker before continuing. "Now," he said, "we come to the fourth block—the block which ensures a gain, or, as we have just seen, a loss. The block against the inside backer-up. In this instance—against Roberts." He wrote Roberts' name above the position shown on the card.

When he continued, the coach's voice was hard and precise. "You never touched Cohen, Jacobs. And, as a consequence, he had a clean shot at Whittemore."

"I'll say he did," Whittemore murmured.

Jacobs' face flushed and he shook his head. "I got mixed up," he said sheepishly. "I went for Roberts—"

"Roberts is Aker's man," Ralston said softly. "He helped Cohen make the tackle. Neither of you—neither you, *nor* Aker—blocked Roberts out of the play."

Ralston turned to the other half of the touchdown-twin combination. "And you, Aker?"

Aker shrugged. "I missed him, Coach."

There was a long silence. "All right," Ralston said, at last. "We'll run the same play. This time, don't get mixed up, don't go for the wrong man, *and—don't miss!*"

Ralston handed the play card to Nelson and stepped back out of the huddle. "All right, Hilton," he said quietly. "Let's go."

Soapy eyed Chip and winked significantly. Chip nodded. He knew what the redhead was thinking. Coach Ralston had known all along what had been going on in the huddle. . . .

"On the count of three," Chip said. "Ready! Hip!" The team broke out of the huddle and fell into position on the line of scrimmage.

Chip took the ball on the count of three and faked just as he had on the previous play. After handing the ball to Montague, he again headed for Speed. Just as before, Speed backed away from the block. Chip slowed down and turned to see Biggie and Junior Roberts again pulling Whitty to his feet. Jacobs and Aker were sprawled on the ground at the line of scrimmage. Chip started back to the huddle, but the blast of Ralston's whistle brought him to a halt.

"That's it," the lanky coach said sourly. "Three laps and in—"

There was a brief, uncertain pause and then the players started for their laps. Chip and Soapy took off around the field together without a word. When they made the first turn, Chip broke the silence. "Coach knew it all the time, Soapy."

"You mean the trouble in the huddle?"

"Right!"

"He sure did, Chip. I'm glad you kept your head. I would have told off those two troublemakers the first time they opened their mouths."

"It wasn't easy."

The two pals matched long strides and continued on around the field. Behind them, Biggie, Speed, Red, Whitty, and Fireball dug along in dogged pursuit. Chip and Soapy sprinted the last fifty yards and then slowed down to a trot as they finished the last lap and passed in front of Ralston and his assistants.

Nibs Nelson elbowed Sullivan and jerked a thumb toward the other end of the field. "Speed merchants!" he said sarcastically.

Far behind the rest of the squad, Eddie Aker and Jack Jacobs jogged leisurely along. In front of the bleachers they slowed down to a walk. Ralston turned at that instant and saw the two players. He muttered something and blasted his whistle. Aker and Jacobs cast startled glances at the grim coach and then broke into a trot.

Ralston waited until they reached him and then gestured toward the field. "Three *more* laps!" he said sharply. "And I mean *running* laps!"

The two sophomores continued on around the field while the staff of coaches grimly watched. When the two players finished the third lap, the coaches walked slowly toward their cabin.

"*That* might help," Nelson said succinctly.

"It's a start," Ralston said shortly.

"They don't know the plays," Rockwell said softly.

"Then we'll teach them the plays," Ralston said quickly. "And," he continued grimly, "we'll make them or break them—this week!"

CHAPTER 7

VARSITY EXPERIENCE

CHIP looked upfield to the forty-yard stripe where the ball rested on the kicking tee. The Wesleyan players were spaced along the thirty-five-yard line waiting for the referee's whistle to start the scrimmage and his teammates were moving restlessly about in their receiving positions. He was aware without looking toward the side line that Speed, Biggie, Joe Maxim, Ace Gibbons, and Mike Brennan were grouped in front of the State bench. He could hear their yells of encouragement and he knew they were sincere, but he knew also how they felt; he knew how tough it was for a starter to root from the side lines. . . .

He took a long breath and moved back to the goal line. From that spot he could see Jack Jacobs standing on his left, five yards from the side line, and, directly opposite, Eddie Aker on the right side line. The coaches had given the two newcomers a lot of attention the past two days. Maybe that was all they really needed—attention and understanding. . . .

Chip's heart was pounding and his legs felt as if they were made of straw as an official came trotting down the field and took a position on the goal line. Then the referee blasted his whistle and the Wesleyan kicker started slowly forward. The ball was in the air before Chip heard the thump of shoe against pigskin. Then, with the sound, his tenseness vanished.

The ball shot out and up and straight down the middle of the field, straight toward Chip on a high end-over-end arc. He gathered the ball in on the ten-yard line and followed Fireball's broad back up the middle of the field toward the apex of the wedge his teammates had formed. Chip was hit on the thirty but made it to the thirty-five-yard line before he was downed.

There wasn't a sound in the huddle as Chip called for a shift to the right, he himself carrying the ball over right tackle on a keeper play. "Seventeen on three!" he said sharply. "Let's go!"

On the count of three Chip took the ball from Leopoulos, pivoted to the right, and faked to Fireball. The big fullback's arms were crossed in front of his chest and Chip held the ball on his right hip as he faked with his left hand. Then he continued on out along the line prepared for the fake to Aker. But Aker slipped and Chip ran head on into the Wesleyan linebacker.

The referee's whistle stopped the play at the line of scrimmage but that didn't stop the tackler. He carried Chip back five yards and dumped him unceremoniously on the thirty-yard line. Chip was shaken up on the play but he scrambled quickly to his feet and hurried into the huddle.

"My fault, Hilton," Aker said ruefully. "I slipped."

"Forget it," Chip said quietly. "Same formation! Buttonhook pass to Aker! On two— Hip!"

The play was a take-off on the keeper. Once again,

Chip faked to Fireball and continued on out for the fake to Aker. This time, Aker's timing was perfect. Chip made the fake, drifted back, faked a pass toward the right side line, and then hit Aker on the State forty-five-yard line just as he buttonhooked back. Aker pivoted and made it to the mid-field stripe before he was downed.

"*That*," Fireball said happily when he reached the huddle, "was a pass!"

"Formation left," Chip said calmly. "Twenty-four on two! That's you, Fireball! Draw play! Straightaway! Hip!"

Chip took the ball on the "two" count, pivoted to the left, and slipped the ball under Fireball's arms. Then he continued on out along the line, faked to Jacobs, and faded back as if to pass. When he looked back, Fireball was down on the Wesleyan thirty-eight-yard line. A twelve-yard gain . . .

Chip could almost feel the confident exultation which now emanated from his teammates. This was the first varsity experience for seven of the players on the offensive platoon. Counting himself, only Soapy, Whitty, and Fireball had played varsity ball. Aker and Jacobs seemingly had blended in with the rest of the newcomers and there wasn't a sound when he called the play.

"Formation left! Thirty-eight on one! That's you, Jacobs. Hip!"

He faked to Fireball, slipped the ball to Jacobs, and once more faded back to fake the pass. The sophomore halfback went into the line at full speed but was hit hard after a two-yard gain. Jacobs got slowly to his feet and cast a surly glance at Ryan and Whittemore as he took his place in the huddle. But he said nothing.

"Same shift," Chip said confidently. "Pass play 190. Montague across! Hip!"

Chip faked to Fireball and then continued on out to the left for the fake to Jacobs. From his position five yards behind the line, Jacobs should have screened into the line at the precise moment Chip arrived for the fake. But just as it had been with Aker, Jacobs was slow. Chip arrived too soon for Jacobs' slow screen and the Wesleyan right end, tackle, and backer-up found it unnecessary to concentrate on Jacobs and a possible thrust through the line. Instead, they rushed Chip and chased him back for a ten-yard loss. Chip had to "eat" the ball and ended up flat on his back on the Wesleyan forty-six-yard line for a ten-yard loss. He got slowly to his feet and walked thoughtfully back to the huddle.

"I was in the clear," Montague said uncertainly.

"I know, Monty," Chip said. "I couldn't get the ball away."

"What happened?" Fireball asked.

"Nothing," Chip said quietly. "All right, now. Same shift. Buttonhook to Jacobs. On the two count."

The pass called for the same fakes and ball handling as in the previous play. This time, everything clicked. Fireball faked beautifully as he cut ahead of Chip, and Jacobs screened Chip with perfect timing at the line of scrimmage. Chip faded back and hit Jacobs on the Wesleyan thirty-yard line just as the left halfback buttonhooked back.

Jacobs circled, and picking up a block from Whittemore, headed for the goal line. But just when it looked as if the speeding pass receiver might go all the way, he turned to look back. The turn broke his stride just enough to enable the Wesleyan safety man to make a desperate dive tackle, and his clutching

hands brought Jacobs crashing to the ground. And—
Jacobs fumbled!

There was a wild scramble for the ball and a pile-
up of churning bodies. The umpire dug down into
the pile of players and then patted a Wesleyan jersey.
It was Wesleyan's ball, first and ten, on their own
twelve-yard line and Ralston sent in his defensive
platoon for the first time. Despite the fumble, the
State fans gave Chip and his teammates a big hand
as they trotted off the field.

Chip took off his helmet and dropped down on the
bench between Soapy and Fireball. Something about
the play of the touchdown twins was beginning to
ring a bell. . . .

"Tough break!" Fireball said shortly.

"Yeah," Soapy agreed. He elbowed Chip. "By the
way, Chipper, what went wrong with the seventeen
play and the 190 pass?"

"Bad timing."

Soapy's eyes shot toward Aker and Jacobs who
were standing on the side line. "Yeah," the redhead said, nodding his head vigorously, "wasn't it,
though?"

There was plenty of room on the bench but the
touchdown twins remained standing, holding their
helmets and turning from time to time to scan the
bleachers. "Must be waiting for someone to ask them
for their autographs," Soapy growled.

"Autographs!" Fireball repeated. "Those two char-
acters will be has-beens before they've ever *been!*"

"They always spoke well of you," Chip said lightly.

Fireball grunted. "Huh! They never spoke well of
anybody."

Wesleyan put the ball into play then and conversation ceased. The visitors were operating from the

single wing and tried the best play in football—the
off-tackle smash. The Wesleyan left halfback took a
direct pass from center and angled for the hole. But
he didn't get far. Biggie and Mike Brennan tossed the
blockers aside as if they were pillows and smashed
the runner to the ground for no gain.

The Wesleyan quarterback tried a pass in the flat
which Ace Gibbons knocked down, a spread play
which gained two yards, and then sent his team into
punt formation. Speed Morris and Gary Young
trotted back to the center of the field and waited for
the kick.

Standing on his own four-yard line, the Wesleyan
kicker barely got the ball away. But it was a good
kick, a high, lazy floater which went spinning high
above Young's head. Gary took a quick look at the
charging ends and the rest of the converging players
and then signaled for a fair catch. Speed backed him
up, shouting words of encouragement. Chip glanced
up at the wobbly ball and then concentrated on
Young. The little sophomore was watching the de-
scending pigskin as if hypnotized, swaying slightly as
he concentrated on the ball.

"He's going to drop it," Chip said, gripping Soapy's
arm.

"Speed!" Soapy yelled. "Heads up!"

The ball took one last swerve and shot over Young's
head. Gary moved back but he was off balance and
couldn't hang on to the ball. It went spinning and
bounding away toward the coffin corner, with Speed
in swift pursuit and the Wesleyan players on his heels.

It looked as if the ball might go out of bounds on
the ten-yard line, but the Wesleyan players were so
close that Speed decided not to take a chance. He
dove headlong and curled his body safely around the

elusive ball on the State seven-yard line. Ralston had Chip and the offensive team on its way almost as soon as the referee's whistle killed the play.

Keyed up by the unexpected break, Wesleyan was determined to keep State pinned back against the goal. So, when State came out of the huddle, the visitors deployed quickly into a 5–4–2 defense. Chip had called for a draw play, with Fireball carrying up the middle. Now he was tempted to use a check signal and change to a pass play, but he let it go and Fireball barely made a yard. Second down, nine yards to go . . .

Back in the huddle, Chip studied the visitors' defensive captain. "They're set for a running play," he muttered, half to himself and half to his teammates. "Just what we want. Heads up, now. Straight-T formation. 91 X pass on the fake draw. Count of one. Whitty and Monty up the side lines. Keep going now. The pass will be to the outside. Let's go!"

He took the ball from Leopoulos on the count of one, faked to Fireball, and dropped back in the pocket for the pass. Whittemore and Montague drove straight upfield for five yards and then on out and up the side lines. Fireball buttonhooked behind the Wesleyan middle guard, and Aker and Jacobs formed the pass-protection pocket with Soapy and O'Malley.

Ordinarily the pocket gave Chip plenty of time to get set for a pass. Soapy and O'Malley did a good job this time, too. But the Wesleyan ends drove through and over Aker and Jacobs as if they weren't there. Chip was concentrating on the receivers but the touchdown twins' weak blocking effort was obvious. They dove under the charging ends, rolling ineffectively along the ground. Chip had no time to pass, barely had time to cover the ball with his arms before he was snowed under by the rush of the big wing men and dropped savagely on the State two-yard line. Third down, fifteen yards to go . . .

Chip had been dumped hard by the big ends but it wasn't the force of the tackle which stunned him. It was the sudden realization that Aker and Jacobs were outsmarting him, that they were cleverly camouflaging their intention to sabotage every play in which they did not carry the ball or catch a pass. And they *meant* to make him look bad in the process. . . .

On his way to his position in the huddle he thought it through. During the past two days the touchdown twins had completely reversed their attitudes. They had kept quiet in the huddle, had mastered the plays, and had carried out their assignments to the letter. Aker and Jacobs had fooled the coaches, all right. And, Chip reflected ruefully, they had fooled him, too.

With the ball resting on the State two-yard line, Chip's teammates had formed the huddle deep in the end zone. There had been some talking while they assembled but all conversation ceased when he took his position. Chip was bitterly angry, now. Football was a team game. If a fellow wanted to play on his own he ought to go out for an individual sport; for tennis or fishing or golf or hunting. One thing was for sure— He had fallen hook, line, and sinker for the cunning duplicity of the touchdown twins.

CHAPTER 8

HIDDEN-BALL PLAY

CHIP didn't know what to do. Right then, he was gripped by a feeling of frustrated anger. Worrying about the opponents and the plays was enough. But when a quarterback also had to worry about a couple of halfbacks pulling fake blocks it was *too* much.

There was time for one more play before the end of the half and Chip didn't know whether he should risk the danger of a safety or kick. "You've got to kick," he told himself. He looked up to see the determined faces of Fireball and Soapy. And just like that, he changed his mind. He thought through his catalogue of plays and chose the most daring one on the list.

"That's it!" Chip breathed to himself. "Aker and Jacobs can't possibly mess it up. They're not even near the ball."

Chip knew he could count on Fireball and Soapy. The play he had in mind called for a good fake by the burly fullback and much depended on a good block by Soapy. He glanced straight at Aker and then eyed Jacobs. "All right," he said grimly, "let's have some blocking from you fellows *this* time— Formation right! Eighteen with a keeper! Four count! Let's go!"

When he was in position behind Leopoulos, Chip started his count and took the ball on four. Then he faked with his left hand and held the ball on his right hip with his right hand. Fireball faked beautifully, thrusting his crossed arms over Chip's hand as if it were the ball, and then drove into the line as if his life depended upon a five-yard gain.

"Now for it," Chip breathed. He forced himself to pivot slowly to the right, transferring the ball at the same time from his right to his left hand. He held the ball on his left hip, out of sight of the visitors' charging linemen. He saw Soapy pull out of the line and start to the left as Whittemore pinned the visitors' big right tackle.

Soapy cut just outside the Wesleyan tackle who was blocked by Whittemore, and Chip continued on, trotting leisurely. When he reached the scrimmage line, Soapy cut swiftly across in front of him and headed upfield. Now, Chip discarded all pretense, pulled the ball up under his arm, and followed Soapy at full speed.

"Bootleg play!" the Wesleyan safety man yelled, dashing toward Chip. "Watch the quarterback!"

Soapy dropped the right backer-up and Chip sped toward the center of the field. It was the right move, because Montague had cut across from his position on the right side of the State formation and was dashing at full speed for the Wesleyan quarterback who was playing in the safety position. Chip slowed his pace enough to let Montague get in the lead and then reversed his field as the tall end timed his block and cut the safety man's feet from under him.

Chip could only see daylight ahead of him now and he stretched his long legs and headed for the

Wesleyan goal line, sixty long yards ahead. Behind him, Chip could hear pounding feet but he didn't look back; he concentrated on a straight line to the opposite end of the field. As he passed the mid-field stripe he heard a tremendous shout from the stands. That told him that one of the visitors was closing the gap or was close enough to make a try for him, and Chip called upon all his speed.

He never saw the Wesleyan left halfback dive for him but he sensed that the danger was past when he flashed across the Wesleyan forty. The crowd noise died down as he cut across the thirty, the twenty, and the ten. But it picked up again when he crossed the goal line for the first score of the game.

He tossed the ball to the official and breathed a deep sigh. The half was over and all he had to do now was kick the extra point or elect to try a two-point running or passing play. Then his teammates ganged up on him, slapping him on the back and punching him good-naturedly.

Chip was still breathing hard but he felt as though a great weight had been lifted from his chest. The gamble had paid off and he felt sure that Aker and Jacobs now realized that he was aware of their trickery. The huddle incident must have brought that home to them. Now he could fight fire with fire.

The referee's whistle sounded and Chip called for a place kick. "Fireball, you hold the ball," he said softly. He paused for a moment and then looked straight at Aker. "Block their left end this time, Aker—"

The eyes of the two players locked. Then Aker shifted his glance and Chip turned his attention to the other member of the touchdown combination. "The right end is your man, Jacobs," he said pointedly. "Stay on your feet."

Not a player moved. Chip waited a second longer. "All right, Leopoulos—" he said. "Pass the ball on the count of two! Let's go!"

Wesleyan was lined up on the other side of the ball, and as soon as his teammates were in position, Chip stretched the kicking tape in line with Fireball's position and the goal.

The ball came back on the "two" count and Fireball plunked it down on the line Chip had drawn across the tape. But it was the first time the big fullback had held the ball for an extra-point kick and his fingers slipped off the ball just as the toe of Chip's kicking shoe crashed through. Chip got the ball up in the air, all right, but it was wide of the mark. The score at the half: State 6, Wesleyan 0.

Coach Ralston devoted the entire intermission to the offense. It was evident that he was disturbed by State's inability to move the ball. When time was up he called on Chip to kick off the defensive platoon.

Chip placed the ball on the kicking tee and glanced along the thirty-five-yard line at Biggie, Speed, Red, Eddie Anderson, Mike Brennan, Ace Gibbons, and Joe Maxim. Only Soapy, Fireball, and Whitty were missing from last year's championship team.

The referee blasted his whistle and, starting slowly forward, Chip picked up his teammates' strides and booted the ball. The wave of players headed downfield after the ball as if pulled by a string. The kick was high and carried to the five-yard line. Chip, playing safety, followed slowly behind the wave of tacklers.

Up ahead, Biggie and Ace Gibbons raced side by side through the Wesleyan blockers and dropped the ball carrier so hard on the fifteen-yard line that he fumbled the ball. But Wesleyan recovered and it was their ball, first and ten, on their own twelve-yard line.

Ralston sent Gary Young in to replace Chip when the referee's whistle killed the ball. As soon as the fans saw Chip give the little quarterback a pat on the back and start for the State bench, they gave him a round of applause.

Ralston met Chip at the side line and grasped his arm. "You pulled us out of a bad hole in the first half, Chip. Nice going!"

"I had a lot of help, Coach," Chip said quickly.

"I know," Ralston agreed blandly. "By the way, weren't you having trouble in the huddle? Some unnecessary talking?"

"No, sir. Not a bit."

"Everyone know the plays?"

"Yes, sir."

"Er, how about the blocking?"

"It could be better, sir."

Ralston nodded grimly. "I know—"

A roar from the bleacher fans drew their attention back to the field just in time for them to see the ball sail over Gary Young's head, light on the fifty-yard line, and roll end over end to the State six-yard line. The visitors had surprised the sophomore field general with a quick kick.

"Back you go," Ralston said, releasing Chip's arm. "Report for Young. Kick it right back."

Chip reported to the official and joined his teammates in the huddle. "Beat it!" Ace Gibbons said, grinning. "Haven't you made a mistake? This is the defensive platoon. Or is the coach mixed up?"

"Coach isn't mixed up," Chip retorted. "He said to kick it right back."

"Oh, no," Speed moaned. "Can't we run the ball just once?"

"Coach's orders," Chip said. "Heads up, now! Kick formation! Ball on three! Hip!"

They broke out of the huddle and Mike Brennan stood poised over the ball until his teammates were set. Chip had moved back until he was standing in the middle of the end zone. He checked the positions of his teammates and started the count. "One, two, three, fo—"

Chip could have counted to ten and still have had plenty of time to kick the ball. Not a Wesleyan player broke through the kicking pocket. And Mike Brennan's pass was, as always, a beauty. The ball came back in perfect position, straight into Chip's outstretched hands and a little to the right. There wasn't the loss of a second as Chip took his stride and slanted a low, powerful spinner toward the side line. The ball took off as straight as a string and sailed out of bounds on the Wesleyan forty-five-yard line.

The referee's whistle killed the ball and Gary Young came racing in to replace Chip. Again Chip got a hand from the stands as he ran off the field. The Wesleyan quarterback tried a running play which was smeared at the line of scrimmage, and then went back to his kicking game; punting on second down. Once again, the visitors' fullback responded with a superb effort, sending a high, wobbly punt almost to the State goal line. The Wesleyan ends were right on top of Speed when he called for a fair catch on the seven-yard line. As soon as Speed caught the ball, Ralston waved his arm and Chip and the offensive team dashed out on the field.

Chip's thoughts had raced ahead, and when he faced his teammates in the huddle, he had his campaign planned. State had run roughshod over Wesleyan the previous season to win by a score of 40 to 14 and it was obvious to every State player on the field that the visitors remembered the beating. They were playing as hard and as desperately as if it were a regularly scheduled game and victory meant the conference championship. Chip wanted another touchdown. Quick! Six points wasn't much of a lead. . . .

He glanced at the visitors' defensive huddle. They had been using a 5–4–2 defense. Maybe he could tighten it up a bit more . . . "All right, formation left! Play 24! Cross buck by Finley! On two!"

Fireball came through with a four-yard gain putting State on their own eleven-yard line, second down and six. Chip flipped a short over-the-line pass to Montague for a gain of five yards to make it third down with a yard to go and then called on Fireball again. The big fellow's carry was good for three yards and the first down.

With the ball resting on the State nineteen-yard line, he went deep into his repertory of plays and came up with a take-off on the keeper he had used on his touchdown run. "Formation right!" he said sharply. "Pass play 96! Fake bootleg option! On the one count!"

Leopoulos passed the ball on the "one" and Chip faked to Fireball, and then pivoted around and hid the ball on his hip as he had done on the touchdown sprint. This time, however, the Wesleyan right end wasn't taking chances; he concentrated on Chip, and was easy pickings for Soapy. The redhead pulled out of the line, and instead of cutting upfield, he drove hard for the big end and cut him down as if by a giant scythe.

As soon as Soapy blocked the end, Chip faded back and looked for his pass receivers. Jacobs and Aker were running down the right side of the field and Montague had cut across in back of the line of scrimmage. Whittemore had thrown a fake block at the Wesleyan right tackle and had then continued down the middle of the field. Just as Chip dug his right foot in the ground and poised to make the throw, Whittemore cut abruptly to the left and raced along the side line.

Chip gauged the distance between Whittemore and the Wesleyan safety man and let the ball fly. He breathed a sigh of relief when he saw that Whitty's long legs were pulling him away from his opponent. "It's going to be close," Chip muttered.

But it wasn't close. Whittemore was six inches taller than the defender, and, without breaking stride, reached above the safety man's hands and pulled in the ball. He kept right on going up the side line, easily outdistancing the safety man, and went all the way for the touchdown. Seconds later, Speed raced in to report for Fireball and Chip dropped back to try for the extra point.

The ball came twirling back and the rest was automatic. Speed plunked the ball down on the tape in perfect position and Chip caught it just right. The ball went flying end over end between the uprights to make the score: State 13, Wesleyan 0.

Ralston sent in the defensive platoon right after the referee raised his arms over his head. And, once again, Chip kicked off. This time, he gave the boot a little extra power and the ball lit in the visitors' end zone and rolled out of bounds. Gary Young replaced Chip and Wesleyan had time for one more play, a desperation pass which Speed knocked down to end the game.

Chip had been sitting on the bench beside Soapy. When the game ended, they trudged wearily through the crowd of spectators who had flowed down out of the bleachers and out on the field. Eddie Aker and Jack Jacobs followed slowly behind them, unnoticed by the two pals. Someone tapped Chip on the arm and he looked up to see Skip Miller.

"Nice going, Chip," the high school star said. "You were great!"

"Nonsense! Oh, this is my best pal, Soapy Smith. Soapy, this is Skip Miller." Soapy had been staring in openmouthed amazement at Skip. "Holy smokes," he said weakly. "Holy smokes! Am I seeing double?" He shook his head and gulped as he sized up the tall youngster. Then he extended his hand and shook his head again. "I never thought I would see the day—"

"Oh— I forgot!" Skip said. He pulled a magazine from his pocket and thrust it into Chip's hands. "Take a look! It just hit the stands! Look at the cover!"

Chip gazed in surprise at the full-page head shot of a football player. "Why, it's—"

He was startled by a gale of laughter directly behind him. "That's right!" Eddie Aker managed. "It's Chip Hilton—"

"Yeah," Jack Jacobs added. "A new comic magazine!"

CHAPTER 9

CHOOSE OUR FRIENDS

SKIP turned in shocked surprise to face Eddie Aker and Jack Jacobs. "What do you mean?" he asked.

Aker pointed to the magazine. "The comic," he said. "You know— The All-America quarterback." He paused and hooked a thumb at Chip. "States' gift to football."

Skip's face was a picture of puzzled surprise. "You're kidding!"

Aker's face sobered and he glanced from Skip to Chip and back again to the tall high school star. "Hey," he cried, "what's your name? Hilton?"

Skip shook his head. "No, my name is Miller."

"That's good," Aker said. "It's bad enough to look like him."

"You're sure your name isn't Hilton," Jacobs said.

"I'm sure."

"They're great kidders, Skip," Soapy said sourly. "Especially about football. They think they're football players."

"I don't understand," Skip said uncertainly. "Aren't you fellows on the same team?"

"Oh, we're on the same team, all right," Jacobs said. "But you would never know it."

"That's right," Aker added. "The great man, here, the great Hilton, only knows two kinds of plays. His own and those of his friends. He passes everyone else up—"

"When did I pass you up?" Chip asked calmly.

"Lots of times," Jacobs said angrily.

"If you want to be specific," Aker said, "on that last pass play."

"And on every play since you got dumped on the goal line," Jacobs added.

Soapy moved over in front of the touchdown twins. "He got dumped because you fellows didn't do any blocking," he said accusingly.

"They faked the blocks, Soapy," Chip said. He nodded at Aker and continued, "I'll admit you fellows surprised me with your clumsy imitations, but it didn't have anything to do with that last pass. You were both covered. Whitty wasn't."

"Naturally," Jacobs drawled. "Haven't you been reading the papers, Lefty?"

"No! Why?"

"Then you don't know about State's All-America passing combination—Hilton and Whittemore?"

"Well, I haven't been doing much reading," Aker said pointedly, "but I happen to know that Hilton and Whittemore work together at State Drug."

"What's that got to do with it?" Chip demanded.

"Just buddy-buddy," Aker said. "You know— buddy-buddy, palsy-walsy. On the field and off the field."

Chip smiled and nodded agreement. "You're right, Aker," he said coolly. "Coach chooses the team but we can choose our friends. See you around."

"We'll be around, Hilton," Jacob said darkly.

"Don't forget your clippings for the next scrimmage game," Soapy said. "These guys today didn't know who you were."

Aker and Jacobs turned away glowering and muttering.

Chip, Soapy, and Skip continued on their way. Skip whistled softly in relief. "Nice guys," he said thoughtfully. "I'm glad they're not on my team."

"Team!" Soapy echoed. "Huh! They don't know what the word means."

"I know," Skip said, nodding. "I saw what happened."

"I hope Coach Ralston saw it," Soapy said grouchily.

"Don't worry about that," Chip said. "Coach doesn't miss much."

"I've got to be going," Skip said. "Sure glad to have met you, Soapy. Oh, yes— Don't forget the job."

"I won't, Skip."

Skip walked swiftly away, and Chip and Soapy studied the front page of the magazine. The picture was in color and presented a full head shot of Chip wearing a white helmet with the familiar blue stripe over the top and down the front.

STATE'S ALL-AMERICA QUARTERBACK ON THE SPOT

"What's that all about?" Soapy asked belligerently, reaching for the magazine. He opened it and leafed through the pages until he came to another picture of Chip. This was an action shot and showed Chip passing in the A. & M. game.

Soapy punched a finger into the page. "*That's* football!" He scanned the pages as they walked slowly toward their cabin.

Reading the magazine, Soapy lagged behind and

Chip walked on ahead. He opened the door and his pals met him with a chorus of good-natured gibes and jeers.

"Chip Hilton is on the spot!" Whitty cried.

"What big feet you have, Cinderella," Red chortled.

"They'll be pointing for the triple-threat star," Fireball chirped.

Speed shook a magazine in the air. "It says here that the Houdini of the gridiron is so clever at concealing the ball that he often forgets where he hides it. How about that?"

Chip made a grab for the magazine. "Come on, Speed—"

"There's more of them," Speed protested. "Bill Bell brought out a carload and gave 'em to everyone."

"He would," Chip groaned.

The kidding lasted while Chip and his pals were showering, but it ended when they reached the dining room. Ralston called skull practice right after dinner, and two hours later when the meeting broke up, the Statesmen were too tired to think of anything except rest and sleep.

Sunday passed pleasantly enough for Chip and his pals. Chip went to church in a nearby village with Soapy and Speed in Coach Nelson's car and spent the rest of the day reading and resting. Monday, right after breakfast, the squad was assembled for a brief meeting.

"This is the last week of camp," Ralston said softly. "And, as you know, we play Mercer in a breakup game on Saturday. Right after the game you are free to leave with your parents or friends. A school bus will take the rest of you to University.

School starts on the following Monday, so this is an important week in our football plans. I promise you a week of action. . . ."

The action started as soon as they reported to the practice field and continued on through the day and into the evening. And it was the same all day Tuesday. Wednesday afternoon, following the warm-up drill, Ralston waved them to the empty bleachers.

"This scrimmage is going to be different," the tall coach said evenly. "It's almost time we separated the men from the boys and we're going to shift all of you from offense to defense and vice versa. We'll start out with the offensive platoon kicking off to the defensive platoon. Let's go!"

"This is it," Chip breathed. "Now I'll really find out if Aker and Jacobs are going to play ball."

He placed the ball in his favorite position on the kicking tee and backed up to the thirty-yard line. He glanced from left to right and from right to left along the thirty-five-yard line where his offensive platoon teammates were standing in readiness. Whitty, Ryan, O'Malley, Leopoulos, and Jacobs were on the left of the ball and Soapy, Logan, Montague, Aker, and Fireball were on the right.

Ralston blasted the whistle and Chip started slowly forward, picked up the wave of blockers, and plunked his tee into the ball. The pigskin flew end over end down to the five-yard line and into the eager arms of Ace Gibbons and the big halfback raced up the middle of the field behind the wedge. Most of Chip's teammates had been dumped unceremoniously before they got near the ball carrier, but Fireball and Soapy broke up the wedge and Chip knifed through for the tackle.

That first big gain was only the beginning. Chip

was playing in the third line of defense but he was making half of the tackles. Aker and Jacobs were blocked out of every play and the green offensive platoon line just couldn't stand up against the hard-driving blocks of the veterans. The defensive platoon scored in seven plays. Then, to add insult to injury, Gibbons kicked a perfect placement to put his team out in front, 7 to 0, after little more than four minutes of play.

Chip chose to receive and big Mike Brennan booted the ball straight to him on the goal line. He darted forward and glanced up ahead at Ryan, O'Malley, Leopoulos, Soapy, and Logan. The five linemen were supposed to drop back from the re-straining line to help with the wedge but they weren't fast enough. Biggie, Maxim, Schwartz, Brennan, and Roberts bore down on him like runaway tanks. Chip didn't have a chance; he was ganged on the twelve-yard line and buried under a pile of tacklers. No quarter asked or given here.

He tried Fireball up the middle on a draw play and the big fullback barely made two yards. On a keeper from formation right, Aker was slow coming up to the line and Cohen, Horton, and Brennan charged through Montague and Logan and met him before he reached the line of scrimmage. He tried an end-around play, Montague to Whitty, and the big end was thrown for a three-yard loss. Aker dove into the line and fell to his knees while Jacobs made a try for Cohen and slipped under the big tackle's hands without even making contact.

Chip was sick at heart. The touchdown twins knew the plays, all right, but they weren't going to help anyone except themselves.

Chip called for kick formation and—just as it had

been in the Wesleyan game—Aker and Jacobs failed to block the charging ends. Horton and Red were on top of him, hands stretched high, when he booted the ball. He barely got the kick away.

Speed took the ball at mid-field and raced clear back to the offensive platoon's thirty, where Chip and Fireball teamed up to make the tackle. On the next play, Gary Young passed over Aker's head to Schwartz and Red scored standing up. Ace Gibbons booted a perfect placement and the defensive platoon led, 14 to 0.

Chip turned back upfield, eyes blazing, anger in his heart. Soapy, Fireball, Whitty, and Leopoulos trudged silently beside him. Chip didn't even see Ralston, nearly walked into him. The head coach was standing on the fifty-yard line, smack in the center of the field.

"Hold it right here, fellows," Ralston said, windmilling his arms to the rest of the players. "I want to make a few changes."

The bench reserves and the two teams on the field ran up and surrounded the tall coach and waited quietly. "There ought to be some way to make the plays go," Ralston said evenly. "Suppose we try a few substitutions—Brennan for Leopoulos, Cohen for Ryan, Maxim for Logan, Morris for Jacobs, and Gibbons for Aker. That's it! On the double now!"

Chip sprinted for his receiving position in front of the goal. This was more like it. . . .

Leopoulos booted the ball, and Finley, standing on the twenty-yard line directly in front of Chip, took it on the dead run. The speedy fullback was brought down on the forty-yard line and hustled back into the huddle. "Duck soup!" he said jubilantly.

"Right!" Soapy added. "We'll kill 'em!"

Jacobs brought his knee up in a vicious kick

Chip called formation right and the end-around reverse. He took Mike Brennan's pass on the count of two, faked to Fireball, then to Ace, slipped the ball to Monty, and headed out for his block. As he rounded right tackle, he saw Whitty take the ball from Monty and race toward him. Up ahead, Jacobs saw Chip coming and advanced warily.

Timing his block, Chip faked with his head to bring Jacobs' hands up and then ducked under them for a cross-body block. Jacobs had reached out with his hands to fend off the block, but once Chip committed himself to his move, Jacobs made no further effort to use his hands. Instead, he took a short step forward and brought his knee up in a vicious kick which landed flush on Chip's jaw.

Chip never finished the block; he fell heavily to the ground. On the verge of a knockout, he was still intent on completing the block and instinct brought him scrambling to his feet. But his head was swimming and he had to drop down on one knee.

"What's the matter with you, Hilton?" Jacobs snarled. "Out of your head? The whistle killed the play— Can't you hear?"

Chip focused his eyes on Whitty and a pile of tacklers unscrambling themselves up ahead on the defensive platoon's forty-yard line. Then he nodded uncertainly. There was no doubt of it. Jacobs was right. The whistle *had* blown. . . .

"How do you like it?" Jacobs continued. "How do *you* like being on the receiving end? I guess *that* will hold you!"

CHAPTER 10

BOOTSIE TREATMENT

MURPH KELLY seemed to be weaving about in front of him and Chip raised a hand to steady the moving figure. It seemed to Chip, then, that Kelly held still long enough to thrust an ammonia stick under his nose. The sharp scent bit through the fog, and, despite Kelly's restraining hand, he struggled to his feet.

"Give me a hand, here, one of you fellows," the trainer said sharply. "Help him over to the bench."

"I'm all right, Murph," Chip protested. "Just dizzy."

"*I'm* not!" Kelly retorted. "Out you go!"

Biggie and Soapy placed Chip's arms over their shoulders and walked him toward the side line. Murph Kelly followed closely behind, muttering angrily.

Coach Ralston and Henry Rockwell advanced to meet them and exchanged places with Soapy and Biggie. "All right, Chip?" Rockwell asked.

"Sure, Coach, It wasn't anything. I told Murph—"

"Quarterback has charge of the team," Ralston said gently. "Trainer has charge of the injuries."

Chip's face flushed. "Sorry, sir," he said, nodding.

Ralston turned and motioned to Pete March. "Defensive quarterback position, March. Young takes Hilton's place."

Chip sat down on the bench and studied the players on the field as he gingerly worked his chin with his hand. After a few moments he shifted his glance to Jacobs and nodded grimly. Now he knew what he was up against.

He glanced toward the offensive huddle. The players were grouped around Ace Gibbons in a tight circle fifteen yards behind the ball. Gibbons was gesturing with his hands and talking rapidly. Then the referee blew his whistle and the teams trotted up to their positions on the line of scrimmage. Young took the ball from Mike Brennan and pivoted left. Then he whirled on around and headed toward right end and Chip saw that every player on the offensive unit was out in front of the little quarterback. It's a keeper play, all right, Chip mused, but it certainly isn't one of the plays coach gave *me*. . . .

He gazed at the scene in amazement. Then he got it. Every player on the offensive team, except Gary Young, was heading for Jacobs. And, one by one, each took a shot at him. Jacobs was hit five or six times in succession by the blockers, but none of them tried to knock him to the ground. At the end, however, he was really clobbered and knocked to the ground.

Jim Sullivan and Nibs Nelson were standing a few steps away and Chip saw the big line coach nudge Nelson. "They're giving him the bootsie treatment," he said softly.

Nelson nodded. "Good! It doesn't make me mad."

The defensive unit brought Young down on their

own three-yard line, and as soon as the referee's whistle sounded, the offensive players ran back to their huddle. They formed quickly and then turned and dashed up to the line in formation left. "Aker's turn," Chip whispered to himself.

He watched closely as Young pivoted to the right and then swung around to the left. And, just as before, every player on the offensive team converged on the left side of the line and headed for Aker. They got to him, too, gave him the same treatment Jacobs had received. But it ended there. Ralston suddenly realized what was going on and rushed out on the field.

"That's enough!" Ralston bellowed angrily. "Twenty laps! Every player on the field!"

Chip got to his feet and started around the field but Murph Kelly checked him. "Where do you think *you're* going? You come with me!"

Chip shook his head resignedly and followed the garrulous trainer. As Coach Ralston had said, the trainer had charge of the injuries.

In the training room, Kelly examined Chip's jaw carefully. "It's all right," he growled, "but it seems to me that a smart quarterback like you would have enough sense to take care of himself."

"What do you mean?"

"You know what I mean! Aker and Jacobs. *Especially* Jacobs."

"He was my man on the play. It was my block."

"Sure! Sure it was! But a smart boxer never leads with his right."

"I don't understand—"

Kelly grunted skeptically. "You understand, all right. Why couldn't you have used a straight shoulder block? Why turn sideways and leave yourself wide open? Wise up, Hilton. The so-called touchdown twins mean double trouble for you."

"I don't think so, Murph."

Kelly turned abruptly away. "Everybody else thinks so," he said shortly. "From now on, you watch your step. Understand?"

Chip nodded and walked slowly out of the training room and back to his cabin. He stripped and showered, and was resting on his bunk when the rest of his pals arrived.

"Jaw all right?" Whitty asked.

"Sure, Whitty, I'm fine. I tried to run, but Murph wouldn't let me."

"He let us," Soapy moaned, tugging at his soaked jersey. "Some fun! Coach makes us run twenty laps because those two guys want to play dirty football."

"It wasn't so bad," Biggie drawled. "I'd do twenty more laps if I could see those two fakers limping around the field again."

"Did you see the act they were putting on?" Red asked.

"How could you miss it!" Speed said. "Every time they passed Ralston they hobbled as though their legs were broken."

Fireball chuckled. "And Ralston didn't even give 'em a tumble."

"Well," Soapy concluded, "I hope Coach finally separated the men from the boys."

Soapy couldn't possibly have known it, but right then, that was exactly what Coach Ralston and his staff were doing. Ralston was pacing back and forth across the sitting room of the coaching staff cabin and Henry Rockwell, Nibs Nelson, and Jim Sullivan were seated at the planning table.

Ralston checked his pacing and rested his hands on the edge of the table. Then he looked across at Henry Rockwell and shook his head. "It isn't going to work out, Rock."

"It's a pretty big step from the frosh team to the varsity," Rockwell said gently. "Maybe they need a little more time."

Sullivan shifted restlessly in his chair and shook his head. "Time is right!" he said hotly. "That Jacobs ought to have about ten years for what he tried to do to Hilton this afternoon."

"Right!" Nelson added. "We lose Chip and we can kiss this year good-by."

"I know," Ralston said thoughtfully. "Rock, s'pose you get Jacobs and Aker over here for a little chat right after dinner. Try to straighten them out."

Sullivan folded the fingers of his big right hand into a fist and rapped the table. "I'd like to straighten them out," he growled.

A brief smile flashed across Ralston's thin lips. Then he continued in even tones, "We'll go along with them a little longer, but I don't intend to get caught. Starting tomorrow, we'll make sure that our key players can go both ways."

"You mean play both offense and defense," Sullivan said.

Ralston nodded. "Right! We've got two more days before the breakup game on Saturday. Let's pour it on 'em!"

Chip was sitting on the bench in front of his cabin. From the dining room the rattle of dishes and the jumbled sound of voices could be heard all the way to the cabin as his teammates enjoyed the steak breakup brunch. But the sounds barely registered. Chip was thinking back over the past two days of practice.

Aker and Jacobs had ignored him completely and that sure was all right with him. He had learned his lesson. Never again, he vowed, would he be taken in by their trickery.

He glanced toward the field. It was only a little after eleven o'clock, but cars had been arriving steadily for the past hour and the field was nearly surrounded. A big crowd would be on hand at kickoff time. Chip's thoughts jumped ahead to school and Jeff. It would be his third year in the famous old dormitory. Then he thought about his job at State Drug and his boss, George Grayson. He was lucky to have such an understanding employer. . . .

Chip was gripped with a feeling of nostalgia. The breakup game marked another milestone in his college life. There would be only one more State training camp for him, only one more preseason stay at Camp Sundown. His thoughts shifted to his mother back in Valley Falls. He sure wished she could have been here today. Even as he made the wish, he knew it was impossible. Ever since the death of his father, she had worked in the Valley Falls telephone office; had worked up to the position of supervisor. But from her devotion to the job, one would have thought she owned the company. Chip knew the real reason. His mother was determined to keep the family home going and to do all she could to see that he got through college. Someday he would take care of the family responsibilities. . . .

He was still buried deep in thought when he heard his teammates coming out of the dining room. A moment later Murph Kelly appeared on the steps of the camp office and bellowed for them to get going. "Hit the bunks!" the trainer yelled. "Dress at one thirty. On the field at two fifteen."

Chip and his pals entered their cabin for the rest period.

When Murph Kelly roused the squad two hours later, Chip, Speed, and Fireball were already dressed in their game uniforms and waiting to have their ankles taped. A few minutes later Leopoulos joined them and they trotted out on the field for their pre-game kicking practice. The stands were jammed and a car occupied every parking spot around the field. Chip and his kicking buddies loosened up and then began their kicking.

Seconds later, a cheer erupted from the stands and Chip turned to watch the Mercer players dash out on the field. They were wearing gold jerseys and blue pants, and went about their warm-up work in a businesslike manner.

"Big team!" Fireball said shortly.

Before Chip could reply, Ralston called them to the State bench. "We'll start with Brennan, Smith, O'Malley, Cohen, Maxim, Whittemore, and Montague on the line— Hilton, Finley, Morris, and Gibbons in the backfield. Brennan and Hilton act as captains. Take the team down the field and back, Hilton."

Brennan grabbed a ball, sprinted out on the field, and plunked it down on the fifty-yard line. Chip and the rest of the team were right behind him and took their positions. "On three!" he cried. "Ready! One, two, three, four—"

Chip felt the rhythm and the surge of power as the veterans took off on the charging signal. *This was more like it!*

When Chip and his teammates returned, three officials garbed in striped shirts and knickers were waiting in the center of the field.

"All right," Ralston said, "Brennan—Hilton! Get out there for the toss. Receive if you win it. Defend the west goal if you lose."

Chip and Mike matched strides as they trotted out to the center of the field where the officials waited with two Mercer players. After the introductions, the referee turned to the Mercer captains. "Visitors' choice," he said. "Call it!"

The Mercer co-captains chose heads, won the toss, and chose to receive. "We'll defend the west goal," Brennan said. The referee signaled the choices to the spectators while Brennan and Chip shook hands with the Mercer captains. Then the two Statesmen hustled back to the side line where Ralston waited, surrounded by players.

Chip edged into the circle between Aker and Jacobs. Then, as the inner circle of players yelled and clasped hands with Ralston, Aker leaned close to Chip. "Finally got your way, didn't you?" he rasped.

Chip glanced at the disgruntled halfback in surprise. "What do you mean?"

"Rockwell!" Jacobs said, elbowing him sharply in the ribs. "That's what he means. Now tell us you weren't responsible for him havin' us on the carpet—"

"I wasn't."

"Oh, no!" Aker said angrily. "You go cryin' to Rockwell and he gets on our backs and—"

"And your pals get back in the starting line-up!" Jacobs added. "What's the matter, big shot, can't you stand on your own feet?"

CHAPTER 11

ROUGH AND TOUGH

BEFORE he could reply, Ralston's "Let's go!" sent the starting team racing out on the field and Chip dug out for the referee who was waiting with the game ball on the forty-yard line. Chip was shaking with rage. Now they were bringing Henry Rockwell into it! Well, he would show them whether or not he could stand on his own feet.

The official tossed the ball to him and Chip placed it carefully on the rubber tee. Then he turned quickly and headed straight for Speed. "Play safety, Speed!" he said shortly. "I'm going to make the tackle." Before Speed had a chance to protest, Chip back-pedaled to the thirty-yard line and concentrated on the ball.

The referee raised his arm and a burst of cheers from the bleachers shot out toward him. Chip could scarcely wait for the whistle. Then the shrill blast cut through and he started slowly toward the ball. He held back a little and got a little farther under the ball than usual, hoping that he would get a high kick which would carry the ball down to the vicinity of the five-yard line.

The drive of his leg carried him ahead of his teammates and he sprinted at full speed. Evading one blocker after another, he drove straight for the visitors' fullback who had caught the ball on his own five-yard line. Chip fended one more blocker away with his hands and then dove over the last one to drop the runner on the Mercer twelve-yard line.

Chip knew that the crowd's cheer was tribute for the tackle but it didn't mean a thing. He scurried back to the defensive huddle, his face grim and determined.

"5–4–2 defense," Mike Brennan said. "Nice tackle, Chip. Let's get 'em gang! Hip!"

Chip dropped into Ace Gibbons' backer-up position and waved the husky veteran back to the safety position. "Trade positions a couple of times, Ace. O.K.?"

"What's the idea?" Ace asked curiously.

"I want to prove something. I'll trade back on fourth down. All right?"

"Sure it's all right," Gibbons said slowly, scanning Chip's face. He grasped Chip's arm. "Look, Chip! Don't let those guys get under your skin. They're not worth it." He turned and trotted back to Chip's position as Mercer advanced to the line of scrimmage.

Chip was still seething with anger as he moved almost automatically to the right and eyed up the visitors' split-T. The formation was unbalanced to the left and Chip figured the play for an off-tackle smash or an end run. But something about the position of Mercer's left end caught his eye and he moved back a step.

When the center put the ball in play, the big end faked a shoulder block at Maxim and cut out for the side line. Chip raced along, slightly behind the big fellow, anticipating the play. "Side-line pass on the outside," he breathed. "Tough . . ."

The Mercer quarterback faked to the wing back and then fired the ball to the tall end. The pass was angled for the side line so that the tall receiver's body was between Chip and the ball; an ideal pass, tough to defend and almost impossible to intercept.

Chip stretched his long legs and raced for the side line, timed his leap, and stretched his right hand as far as it would go.

The nose of the spinning ball bored into his eager fingers and slipped partly away. But he managed to pull it in and to land in bounds, only inches away from the side line. For a second he had to do a tight-rope dance to get his balance, giving the quarterback a chance to follow his pass. He came racing headlong, but Chip caught him just right with a hard stiff-arm and knocked him to the ground. Two other tacklers spun off him as he drove along the side line, past the fifteen, the ten, the five, and over the goal line. A touchdown!

The cheers of the State fans were still ringing across the field when State broke from their huddle and formed in place-kick formation. Then, with Speed holding the ball, Chip booted the placement and State led, 7 to 0.

The Mercer captain elected to receive and again Chip drove the ball to the visitors' five-yard line. This time, Chip had company when he sprinted down the middle of the field. Fireball Finley and Biggie Cohen were right behind him and the three of them dove at the ball carrier at the same time, dropping him on the fifteen-yard line.

When his teammates broke out of the defensive huddle, Ace slapped him on the back and faded back to the safety position without a word. Chip waited impatiently for the visitors to come out of their huddle, moving restlessly along the line. Mercer came out and formed over the ball with their line unbalanced to the left and Chip shifted to a position behind Joe Maxim. The play was a quick opener over left tackle with the left halfback carrying and Chip met him head-on in the hole, stopping him cold on the line of scrimmage for no gain. Once more, he heard the crowd cheer from the bleachers as he hustled back into the defensive huddle.

"Second and ten, gang," Mike Brennan said tersely. "We've got 'em wired. Let's keep 'em that way. We'll use the 5–3–3 defense. Let's go!"

Ace shouldered Chip as they moved out of the huddle. "I like it back there," he said, grinning. "I hope they punt. If they do and I get the ball, I'll show you some fancy open-field running."

"And I'll be blocking for you and won't be able to see," Chip said lightly.

He moved to the outside position in State's second line of defense and studied the formation. Noting that the formation was still unbalanced to the left, he divided his attention between the quarterback and the end. On the "three" count, the Mercer field general faked to the left halfback on a dive play, to the fullback through the middle, and then dropped straight back. Chip wasn't sure who had the ball because the end passed Maxim up and drove straight for Mike Brennan.

Chip followed the end for two quick strides. Then he saw the left halfback fade out toward the side line. "My zone!" Chip breathed. "And he's wide open!"

Groaning at his stupidity, he followed as fast as he could. The Mercer quarterback had outfoxed him;

had used the big left end as a decoy and he had fallen for it hook, line, and sinker.

"Pass!" Brennan shouted.

It was too late for Chip to get behind the halfback, so he chased him at full speed, watching the speedy runner's eyes. But the halfback was clever; never shifted his gaze. Chip was on the verge of turning his head to locate the ball when he heard Speed's frantic shout. "Chip! Now! Now!"

The warning came just in time. Chip saw the halfback's eyes flash upward and he leaped and turned in the air. The ball was right over his head and he made a desperate stab at the twirling pigskin. It was sheer luck, but his fingers managed to touch the ball just enough to change its course and knock it out of bounds.

Angrily berating himself, Chip trotted back to the State huddle. "Tricked me," he said, glancing around the circle.

"No harm done," Ace said quickly. "You made a good play."

"Thanks to Speed," Chip said, glancing at his buddy.

"All right, all right!" Brennan said sharply. "Third and ten coming up! 6-2-2-1 defense! Drop back, Chip."

Chip nodded his thanks to Ace and hurried back to the safety position on the thirty-five-yard line. But when Mercer came out of their huddle and lined up in punt formation, he backpedaled to the mid-field stripe.

State's hard-charging forwards rushed the kicker, but he managed to get the ball away, angling it toward the left side line. Chip took the ball on the dead run and saw that there was lots of daylight ahead. Speed had dumped Mercer's right end and Fireball had clobbered the center. He sprinted down the left side line and reached the visitors' twenty-three-yard line before he was pulled down. First and ten!

"Are we rolling!" Brennan exulted, when they reached the huddle.

"Heads up, now!" Chip called. "Formation right! Twenty-three draw play! Fireball on two! Hip!"

After slipping the ball to Fireball, he cut back as if to pass. It was a good fake, but when he turned to look, there was a big pile-up at the line of scrimmage. Fireball had run into a stone wall. He cast a quick look at the Mercer linemen as they unscrambled. They were *big, rough, and tough!*

The huddle formed and he called for a pass. "The 90 R with a hook," he said calmly. "That's you, Monty. In the breadbasket on the ten-yard line. On one, gang!"

Chip faked to Fireball diving into the line, cut past Ace and, still concealing the ball, faded back. But the fake didn't work. The Mercer left tackle and left end barreled in at full speed and Chip barely had time to get the ball away. At that, he hit Montague perfectly, drilling a hard, fast pass smack into the lanky end's stomach. But Montague dropped the ball. Third and ten . . .

The ball still rested on the twenty-three-yard stripe, fifteen yards in from the left side line and Chip swiftly figured the angle for a possible placement. He decided to try one more running play. "Formation right! Reverse 59 to the right! Montague to Whittemore. Lots of good blocking now! On three! Hip!"

Again Chip faked to Fireball and Gibbons. Then he slipped the ball to Montague and continued on toward the visitors' left halfback. It was the same play which had brought on the trouble with Jacobs, and Murph Kelly's advice about the use of a straight shoulder block was vivid in his mind. A fake cross-body block with his head and shoulders drew the halfback's hands to Chip's left and Chip drove through with a straight shoulder block which knocked his opponent cleanly to the ground.

The block carried Chip down on top of the half-back, and when he leaped to his feet and twisted around to look for Whitty, he saw that the big end was down on the twenty-five-yard line. Fourth down! And State hadn't gained an inch.

Chip was the farthest Statesman downfield and his teammates stood waiting in the huddle circle. "Kick it, Chip," Brennan urged.

"Right!" Chip said, nodding. "On two, gang! Hip!"

Speed stretched the kicking tape seven yards be-hind the ball on a straight line between the toe of Chip's kicking shoe and the center of the goal and then knelt in the holding position. On the "two" count Brennan's pass came back fast and true and straight into Speed's hands.

Chip took a short forward step with his right foot, then a long left, and met the ball with his kicking toe just as Speed plunked it on the ground. He could have made the kick blindfolded. Nobody, but no-body, could handle the ball for a placement better than the speedy scatback. The ball twirled end over end and straight through the middle of the uprights for three points. State 10, Mercer 0.

The Mercer captain elected to kick and Chip turned to lead the way to the receiving formation just as Gary Young, Aker, Jacobs, and Junior Roberts came trotting out on the field.

Without breaking stride, Chip headed for the bench. Then he heard the applause and shouts and glanced up to see that the fans were standing and yelling and looking straight at him. "Yeah, Hilton!" "Nice going, Kid!" "Atta boy, Hilton!"

Chip cast another quick look and located Skip. His new friend was standing in front of his usual place in the bleachers yelling at him and shaking an exulting fist in the air. Chip ducked down on the bench but the applause and cheers continued until the teams lined up for the kickoff.

Skip was one of the last of the bleacher fans to sit down but that didn't check his enthusiasm. He turned gloatingly to Mr. Aker and Mr. Jacobs. "What did you think of *that* performance?" he demanded.

"What performance?" Mr. Aker repeated. "What did he do?"

"Do? Oh, just kicked off and made the tackle; intercepted a pass and ran for a touchdown; kicked the extra point; kicked off again and helped make the tackle; played in a backer-up position and made the first tackle from scrimmage; knocked down an almost sure pass; ran back a punt for twenty-seven yards, and kicked a field goal. That's all he did!"

"Show-off!" Mr. Aker said sourly.

Coach Bill Carpenter and Mr. Blaine had scarcely spoken to the two men up until now. But Carpenter couldn't resist the temptation to join the conversation. "That's right," he agreed blandly. "He sure did show off. He showed what an All-America quarterback can do. Now we'll see what *your* kids can do."

CHAPTER 12

GOLDEN OPPORTUNITY

"OUR KIDS will do all right," Mr. Jacobs said hotly. "Trouble is, they don't call the plays like Hilton does."

"No one does that," Skip said, grinning.

"Hilton never gives our kids a chance!" Aker growled. "He *never* calls their signals."

"Hilton isn't calling the signals *now*," Mr. Blaine said calmly.

"Right!" Jacobs agreed. "Now you'll see some team play. Young called the plays for the frosh team last year and I guess *they* did all right."

"Sure did!" Aker added. "Won every game!"

"Hilton tries to do *everything*," Jacobs rasped. "Always puttin' on a show, tryin' to do everything himself."

"Mark my words," Aker said. "Young will make everyone forget Hilton if Ralston gives him a chance. We've seen him work."

Carpenter burst into a gust of laughter. "You must be crazy," he said. "Young can't carry Hilton's shoes. He can't run or pass or kick half as well as Hilton. Besides, he's not as big nor as fast or half as smart—

Another thing, Aker, Hilton doesn't *try* to do everything. He *does* everything!"

"But good!" Skip added.

"No, my friend," Carpenter continued, "no one will forget Hilton for a long, long time. Skip, here, is tops in our league and plays a lot of football but he's far from being another Hilton."

"Give him time," Blaine said shortly. "Wait until Skip gets two years of Brand football under his belt, two years under Stew Peterson."

"Chip is more than a football player," Skip said quickly. "He's a top student. Leads his class."

"Our kids aren't dumbbells by a long shot," Jacobs growled. "Hilton hasn't got a monopoly on brains."

"What about your triple-threat triplets?" Mr. Blaine asked pointedly. "First time we met you two men that was all you talked about—Hilton and your kids being the triple-threat triplets."

"Huh!" Aker snorted. "You think Hilton's gonna let anyone touch the ball? Not a chance! We didn't know Hilton then—we know him *now*. Our kids tell us what goes on."

The conversation ended as the Mercer fullback booted the ball. It went hurtling high in the air and down to Junior Roberts on the ten-yard line. There, he was tackled so hard that he had to call for a timeout. Murph Kelly worked on the big fullback for a few moments and then play was resumed.

Young tried an off-tackle slant to the right with Aker carrying for no gain. Then the little quarterback called on Jacobs for a wide end run around the other side of the line. But the sharp blocking of the starting backs was noticeable by its absence and Jacobs was thrown for a five-yard loss back on the fifteen-yard line. Young was desperate and tried a short pass which the Mercer middle guard nearly intercepted. It was fourth and fifteen, now, and State had to kick. The visitors' ends broke through Aker and Jacobs, but Roberts got a good kick away, booting the ball to the Mercer forty-five-yard line. Biggie dropped the receiver in his tracks.

The visitors had learned all they needed to know about State's veteran line by this time so they took to the air. The first pass was in Aker's territory and the visitors' right end went high in the air over Aker's head and came down with the ball on the State thirty-five-yard line. Aker's tackle was late and the end bulled his way for five more yards before he went down.

A short buttonhook in front of Jacobs was good for ten yards and the visitors had the ball on the State twenty. Brennan waited until the huddle formed to call time out and Ralston sent Finley, Gibbons, and Morris racing in for Roberts, Aker, and Jacobs. Chip got to his feet but the coach looked right past him and he sank back on the bench. And he remained there for the rest of the game.

The State veterans' strong defense stalled Mercer's running and passing attack, but without Chip to spark their own offense, the Statesmen could do no more than play the visitors on even terms. There was no more scoring, and when the game ended, Chip joined his pals and walked along with them toward the cabins.

"One of those Mercer guys said I looked like Red Grange," Soapy said smugly.

Speed laughed. "Grange was a back."

"And," Biggie added, "an All-America selection."

"I'd be All-America, too," Soapy growled, "if Ralston used me where I belong."

"Where's that?"

"In the backfield!"

"You can't run fast enough to catch cold."

"Well, anyway," Soapy said loftily, "I look like Red Grange."

"Nuts!" Speed said. "Grange was six-two and could run like a deer. Besides, he was as lean as a greyhound."

"Well," Soapy conceded, "maybe I can't run like Grange could and maybe I'm not a greyhound—"

Speed couldn't let that pass. "You hear that, Biggie," he cried. "Soapy says he's not a greyhound."

"Of course he isn't," Biggie drawled. "He's a chowhound."

That set Speed off in another gale of laughter. Soapy waited grimly until Speed quieted and then continued slowly, choosing his words carefully. "I meant to say that I'm not as lean as a greyhound, but I'm like him—"

"Like a greyhound! Oh, no!"

"No!" Soapy shouted. "Like Red Grange! I wear number 77 and I've got red hair."

Roaring with laughter, Speed and Biggie jumped the redhead and roughed him up all the way to the cabin. Chip had enjoyed the kidding, but he wanted to be ready in plenty of time for the trip to University and hurried into the shower. The rest of his pals followed suit and then hustled their gear outside.

A few minutes later the bus appeared and Soapy grabbed his suitcases. "C'mon, you guys!" he yelped. "Let's go! University, here we come!"

It was a hilarious ride. The end of training camp

had released the players from most of their tension, and since Mr. Aker and Mr. Jacobs had driven their sons home, there was nothing to dampen the enthusiasm of the squad. Soapy took charge, suggesting and leading cheers for everyone in the bus, including the driver. Then he suggested boos for the coaches and the response was so enthusiastic that several of the sophomores riding in the back seat cast apprehensive glances back at the coaches' car which was right behind the bus.

There wasn't much levity in the coaches' car. Curly Ralston was in a glum mood, his attitude clearly expressing his disappointment in the showing of the Statesmen against Mercer.

"They were pretty big," Nelson said tentatively.

"And tough!" Sullivan added. "I hope we don't run into another line like that. Not this season, anyway."

"It wasn't their line," Ralston said gloomily. It was our depth, rather our lack of it. If Aker and Jacobs would only team up with Hilton, we might be able to get by. If they don't—"

"It *could* be a dream backfield," Nelson said.

"You mean nightmare backfield," Sullivan growled. "For Hilton and us, too. I haven't had a good night's sleep since those two birds reported to camp."

"I guess we'll all be glad to get back to University," Rockwell said softly.

Chip glanced at the stockroom clock. Eight o'clock and two more hours to go. It had been a long, long day. His first class had met at a quarter to eight that Monday morning and he had waded through all the hustle and bustle of making classes, meeting old friends, and getting back into the swing of college

life. He was through at three o'clock, and since
Coach Ralston had called off practice, he had hurried
down to State Drug to try to catch up on a whole
summer's accumulation of stockroom problems. His
task was doubly difficult because his assistant, Eddie
Redding, had been given another job.

His thoughts were broken by a loud thump and
Soapy shouldered through the door and dropped
wearily into a chair. "What a crowd!" the redhead
said. "Everybody in town must have been waiting for
us to get back. Why, we weren't as busy as this last
year after the A. & M. game! Oh, my aching back!"

"How about Fireball and Whitty?"

"We're taking turns for a breather. They'll be in as
soon as I rest up. Oh, yes, Skip Miller is out there.
Want to see him?"

"Sure!" Chip said. "Sit still. I'll get him."

Skip was sipping a soda at the end of the crowded
fountain. But he finished his glass with a gulp as
soon as he saw Chip. "Hope I'm not taking you away
from anything," he said nervously.

"You're not," Chip said quickly. "Come on back."

When they reached the stockroom, Skip placed a
piece of paper in Chip's hand. "Trouble," he said,
shaking his head worriedly. "It's a Brand scholarship
blank. Uncle Merton wants me to sign it."

"Scholarship blank?"

"That's right. It's a grant-in-aid for four years of
college."

"Why sign it now?"

Skip shook his head. "I don't know. Uncle Merton
said it had to be in early. What am I going to do?"

"Let's think about it," Chip said, studying the
form.

"Trouble," Skip said *worriedly*

BRAND UNIVERSITY

Application for a Grant-in-Aid or a Scholarship

Dear Sir:

I wish to make application for a grant-in-aid or scholarship at Brand University. If this award is approved, I agree to report for football on the date stipulated by the Conference and Brand University.

It is my understanding from the representative of Brand University who interviewed me that:

1. The grant-in-aid or scholarship awarded by the University will cover (a) tuition (b) fees (c) meals (d) room (e) books (f) $60.00 per month for laundry and incidentals.
2. I understand that any other aid afforded me by school officials, alumni, or friends to attend college or to influence my preference of college is illegal and will destroy my eligibility.
3. If injured while participating in athletics supervised by a member of the coaching staff, the medical expenses will be paid by the athletic department.
4. This grant-in-aid is awarded for four years at Brand University as long as I conduct myself under the rules of the University and make normal progress toward graduation.

. . . .
Signature of Parent *Signature of Applicant*

"That isn't the only one," Skip said, pulling a sheaf of papers out of his pocket. "I've received about sixty letters from coaches all over the country. You must have gotten a thousand!"

"Not quite," Chip said, smiling. "By the way, were all the scholarships the same?"

Skip shook his head. "Oh, *no!* Gosh, some of the

people who talked to me made all kinds of promises. Not coaches. Alumni or fans I guess you would call them. Like Uncle Merton. Some of them promised me a car and two or three hundred dollars a month and a job for my father. One man even said he would see that my family got a house. All paid for— I'm all mixed up."

Soapy had listened without a word. Now, he could stand it no longer. "*You're* all mixed up," he said bitterly. "Heck, you ought to be in *our* shoes! State's touchdown twins have all of us in an uproar."

The stockroom telephone rang then and Chip answered and listened briefly. "Sure," he said. "Right away." He turned to Skip. "I've got some work to do now, Skip. Why don't you hold off your uncle for a week or so? Maybe we can think of something. All right?"

"He's pretty hard to buck, Chip, but I'll try. Er, you didn't have a chance to ask Mr. Grayson about the job?"

"Not yet, Skip. Don't worry. I won't forget."

After Skip left, Soapy went back to the fountain and Chip began to fill the steady stream of orders which came from the various departments of the store. Soapy, Fireball, and Whitty quit at ten o'clock sharp and left for Pete's Place to get a sandwich. But Chip remained on the job, trying to get a head start for the next evening. He was so absorbed in his work that he did not notice his employer standing in the open doorway to the stockroom.

George Grayson was in his fifties. He was tall, slender, and his hair was graying at the temples. He watched Chip quietly for a moment, a slight smile on his lips. "You can't do it all at once—"

Chip was startled. He glanced up quickly and

nodded. "I guess you're right, Mr. Grayson, but I'm pretty far behind."

"I guess you heard about Eddie's promotion."

"Yes, sir. Mitzi told me about it."

Grayson smiled. "Yes, thanks to your training, Eddie is now Mitzi's assistant. Helps her at the cash register. This is his day off. But don't worry, I'll have a replacement in a day or two."

"I know one, Mr. Grayson," Chip said eagerly. "A good one! That is, I think he will be a good one."

"What's his name?"

Chip hesitated. "Why, his last name is Miller. I don't know his first name, but everyone calls him Skip. Skip Miller. He's quite a high school football player and he needs a job. Badly."

Grayson nodded. "Skip Miller. Oh, yes. I've heard of the boy. Where did you meet *him?*"

It was a golden opportunity and Chip seized it quickly. George Grayson was a sports fan. And he liked athletics and liked to have outstanding athletes working for him. But he never exploited their popularity. Nor did he pamper them. Chip held nothing back, now. He told his employer everything he knew about Skip and his predicament.

When Chip finished, Grayson nodded understandingly. "He's in rather a tough spot, isn't he?"

"He sure is, Mr. Grayson."

Grayson studied Chip's anxious face for a brief moment. "Well," he said, "it looks as if Skip Miller has found a true friend." He paused briefly. "And," he added gently, "a job! Tell him to report to work on Monday."

CHAPTER 13

THE WHITE HELMET

Skip caught the box in his long, deft fingers and placed it on the shelf. "Keep 'em coming," he said, grinning.

"Don't worry," Chip said, glancing at the big packing box. "There's plenty more."

When the box was emptied they took a breather. Chip sat down at his desk and Skip stretched out in a chair, sighing contentedly. "This has been a big week in my life, Chip," he said happily. "I never had a regular job before. If I could keep this job I could go to State and help out at home, too. If only Uncle Merton would leave me alone—"

"There's lots of time."

Skip shook his head. "Uh, uh, that's where you're wrong. He keeps after me to sign the contract every time he sees me."

"Well, anyway," Chip said, "the job gives you a measure of independence."

"You can say that again," Skip agreed, grinning. "Pop and Mom are tickled pink."

"How will it feel tomorrow when you get your first check?"

Skip grinned. "Like a million! How will you feel when you line up in the stadium tomorrow afternoon against Templeton?"

"The same way you'll feel next Friday night. Better than a million!"

"Bill Bell wrote in his column in the *Herald* this afternoon that Ralston planned to start the touchdown twins. Is that right?"

"I don't know, Skip. He's been working with them a lot this week."

"Bell said something else," Skip said, eying Chip warily.

"What?"

"He said the fans would be watching for the first State player or players to run out on the field with a ball. Said he or they would be the new State captain or captains. He said that one of the players would be wearing number 44."

"Don't believe everything you read in the papers."

"You'll see," Skip said confidently. "What are you writing?"

"Coach Ralston's new formation," Chip said.

"Mind if I look?"

"Of course not."

Chip had drawn the right and left shifts of the formation and had written in the names of the best players. The only exceptions had been the right end and the two halfback positions.

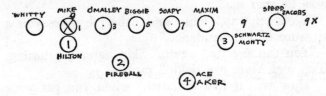

"We're using almost the same formation," Skip said thoughtfully. "I thought Speed and Jacobs alternated in the left-halfback positions—"

"They do," Chip explained. "But that's where Coach Ralston uses his halfbacks. He shifts the left halfback to the right-end position on formation right and his right halfback to the left-end position when the shift is to the left."

"Where does the right end play?"

Chip pointed to Red Schwartz's name. "Right here. A yard behind the line and just off Maxim's right shoulder."

"How about the left formation?"

Chip quickly sketched the formation and wrote in the names. "All right?" he asked.

"I still don't understand why he uses the halfbacks in the end positions," Skip said, shaking his head.

"He sometimes spreads the ends," Chip explained, "and that puts our backs out wide where their speed is important. Besides, the ends are used for the heavy blocking on the running plays and the position a yard back gives them a little more authority when they hit."

"How do you call the plays?"

"By the numbers. The quarterback is number one, the fullback two, the left halfback three, and the right halfback number four. The numbers along the line show the holes— Say, we'd better get busy."

The rest of the evening passed slowly for Chip. Tension was beginning to gather in his chest and he thought the hours would never pass.

The sun was shining brightly the next morning. There was a bit of a wind but it was a perfect football day. He worked feverishly in the stockroom until noon, and when he left for the stadium, he was as nervous as a cat. Murph Kelly and his assistants taped each player quickly and efficiently and then shooed them into the dressing room where their uniforms were laid out on long tables. Chip dressed slowly and carefully, checking each part of his uniform over and over. Just as he finished, Coach Ralston and his assistants appeared and Murph Kelly called the players to order.

"This isn't going to be a pep talk," Ralston said, checking the eager faces of his players. "However, there *is* one important task to be performed before we go out on the field—the selection of a captain or captains. All right, Murph, hand out the pencils and papers."

Chip quickly penciled Ace Gibbons at the top of his paper and Mike Brennan at the bottom and folded it neatly. In a minute or so Murph Kelly collected the papers in a helmet and placed it on the table in front of Ralston. Then, with Rockwell, Nelson, and Sullivan helping him, Ralston sorted the papers.

At the end, there were only four piles of papers. One piece of paper in each of the three and all the others in one big pile. A little smile hovered on the lips of the coach as he faced the squad. "You have chosen only one player as your captain," he said. "He won both leaderships—hands down."

Ralston turned to pick up the familiar white helmet with the blue stripe and held it briefly in his hands.

Then he tossed it quickly and surely into Chip's hands and his "Good luck, Hilton" was lost in a cheer which shook the room.

Minutes later, carrying the ball under his arm, Chip led the starting team out on the field and was met with a deafening roar from the State fans. Chip's heart was thumping so hard that he felt as though he would never get his breath. But the feeling disappeared when he trotted out to the center of the field where the four officials were waiting.

Two Templeton players ran out from the visitors' bench at the same time. The referee took care of the introductions and then turned to the Templeton players. "Visitors' choice, fellows. Heads or tails?"

The taller of the two players said, "Heads." Heads it was, and the same player chose to defend the north goal.

"We'll receive," Chip said.

While the referee was signaling the choices to the stands, Chip shook hands with the visiting captains and wished them luck. Pivoting, he ran back to the circle of players surrounding Ralston.

"All right," the coach said, extending his hand. "We're receiving. Remember, they've got the wind behind them. Good luck!"

Chip and his teammates trotted out to their positions and the roar of the crowd came beating down around him until he couldn't distinguish the State cheers from those of the Templeton supporters. He glanced quickly toward Jacobs on his left and then toward Aker on his right. Now that Coach Ralston was starting them in the first game of the season, he wondered if they would forget their animosity toward him and play ball. Well, it wouldn't take him long to find out. . . .

The referee raised his hand and Chip acknowledged the signal. On the blast of the whistle, the Templeton captain started forward, picked up his line of teammates, and booted the ball high in the air. But he tried to get the ball too far up in the air and it carried only as far as Finley standing on his own twenty-yard line. Fireball took the ball and headed bull-like straight up the middle. And he didn't vary his path an inch, plowing straight away until he went down under a swarm of tacklers on the State thirty-two-yard line.

Chip followed swiftly and was already in the huddle position when Fireball was uncovered by the referee. He wanted to be sure that Aker and Jacobs got the feel of a real game before entrusting them with the ball and called on Fireball for a draw play over right guard. "Formation right! Twenty-three on three!" he said. "That's you, Fireball! Let's go!"

Fireball bulled his way to the thirty-seven-yard line and it was second down, five yards to go. Chip glanced at Aker and met the steady gaze of the right halfback. "Forty-four on two! That's you, Aker! Cross buck! Let's go!"

Chip faked to Fireball with his left hand and held the ball on his thigh with his right hand. As he passed Aker, he gave him the ball and continued on back to his passing position. Aker took the ball at full speed and carried to the forty-three-yard line for the first down. Back in the huddle, Chip smiled at him and nodded his head. "Nice going, Aker."

"Thanks, captain—*sir!*" Aker said, a mocking smile on his lips.

It was all Chip could do to take the thinly veiled insult, but he did it, filing the little incident for future reference. But, even as he called the play, he was thinking that the feud was still uppermost in Aker's mind.

"Heads up!" he said quickly. "Formation right! Thirty-eight on one! That's you, Jacobs, on the reverse. Hip!"

Chip took the ball from Brennan on the "one" count and faked to Finley, to Aker, and slipped the ball to Jacobs as the left halfback raced back out of the right-end position. Jacobs picked up good interference from Soapy and O'Malley and carried to the Templeton forty-five-yard line before he was downed. It was a twelve-yard gain and another first down.

The State fans were rooting the Statesmen on with their "Go!—Go!—Go!" cheer and Chip could hardly make himself heard in the huddle. He called the play and looked around the circle of faces. From their huddle positions directly in front of him, Aker and Jacobs were openly sneering, secure in the fact that no one but Chip could see their faces.

The "I told you so" expressions on the faces of the touchdown twins was hard to take and for a split second Chip was on the verge of telling them off. But, once again, he passed over their animosity and called the play. "Formation left!" he said, covering up the short interlude in his thinking. "Thirty-two on three! That's you again, Jacobs. Cross buck. Hip!"

"Thank you, captain—*sir!*" Jacobs said, smirking and glancing slyly at Aker.

"Check!" Chip cried. "Signals off!" He turned quickly to the referee. "Time!"

CHAPTER 14

THREE PLAYS AHEAD

MOST OF THE STATESMEN had started for the line. They walked back, now, some of them with curiosity written on their faces, others with grim understanding and hope. Soapy, Biggie, Fireball, Whitty, and Brennan were in the latter group. Chip had taken all he could stomach from Aker and Jacobs. This thing was going to be settled right here and now.

He strode into the middle of the circle of players and held up his hand for silence. "Let's get this squared away once and for all," he said grimly. "I didn't ask for it, but you fellows elected me your captain. Besides, Coach told you why the quarterback ran the team—

"From now on, there will be no more wisecracks or talking in the huddle by anyone unless it concerns a play."

Chip paused and moved directly in front of Aker and Jacobs and looked from one to the other as he continued: "As for you fellows, the next time you give me that mister or sir or any other funny stuff— in the middle of the field or in the huddle—*you're* leaving the game or *I* am. Understand?"

The touchdown twins faced up to him for a long second. Then their bravado broke and they nodded sullenly; shifted their eyes and glanced briefly at one another before they stepped back.

Chip took his place in the huddle, angrily aware of the cold hate in the eyes of Aker and Jacobs as they glared at him. "All right," he said, forcing himself to ignore the bitter duo, "same play. Thirty-two on three! Let's go!"

There wasn't a sound from the players as they whirled out of the huddle and hustled up to the line. Chip faked to Fireball, slipped the ball to Jacobs, and dropped back, again faking a pass.

Jacobs cut between Brennan and Montague and carried three yards to the Templeton forty-two-yard line. Second and seven . . .

In the huddle, Chip called for right formation and the pass take-off from the fake cross buck. It worked perfectly. Fireball drove through the line as if he were carrying for a touchdown and Aker did the same. This time, when Chip faded back, he had the ball.

Montague had sprinted out into the right flat and Chip could have hit him. But Jacobs had cut through the line, broken toward the middle of the field, and then headed for the side line. He was in the clear, speeding past the Templeton twenty-yard line. Chip gave him a good lead, aiming the ball for the ten-yard line.

It was a beautiful pass, timed just right, light as a feather and perfectly placed; hard to miss; a perfect touchdown pass. Perhaps Jacobs was too anxious; perhaps he was surprised that Chip would throw to him after the huddle episode. Whatever the reason, Jacobs leaped too soon, got only a piece of the ball, and couldn't hold on to it. The ball flew off his finger tips and right into the hands of the visitors' scatback.

The speedy runner was surprised but he recovered instantly and took off straight up the side line.

Never dreaming Jacobs could miss the pass, Chip had drifted over to the right side line to cover. Now, he groaned and dashed up behind Montague, trying desperately to get into position for a good tackle. But, incredibly fast, three of the Templeton secondary players had formed ahead of the scatback and were leading him up the side line. One of them bowled Montague over as if he were a bag of straw and the other two concentrated on Chip.

He tried to hand-fight them so they would show first, but neither left his feet. The ball carrier reached him, then, and it was now or never.

Chip dove over the first blocker and managed to grasp the runner's jersey. But the second interferer had delayed just long enough and had a clear shot at Chip, and cut him down from the side with a vicious cross-body block just as the runner sped past and headed for the goal line.

Chip was up almost as soon as he was down and gave chase. But the runner was tearing across the fifty-yard line, twenty yards ahead, and it was an impossible handicap. Chip managed to pick up ten of the twenty yards but that was as close as he could get. The ball carrier crossed the goal line to score the first touchdown of the game. Thirty seconds later, the visitors' fullback booted a perfect placement. The score: Templeton 7, State 0.

Chip elected to receive again, disappointed and hurt by the sudden twist of fate which had changed a sure State touchdown into a score for Templeton. But it was past and he waited eagerly for the Templeton kick. The visitors still had the wind behind them and he figured the kick this time would carry all the way to the goal line. He was right. The whistle bit through the crowd roar and the ball was in the air, heading straight toward him.

He shot a quick desperate glance toward the wave of tacklers. Aker and Jacobs made weak attempts to block the rangy ends who converged on him, but the eager Templeton wing men ran over them as if they weren't there. Chip didn't have a chance, barely made it to the twelve-yard line before he was smashed to the ground. First and ten . . .

Chip was furious when he scrambled to his feet. It was the same old story—Aker and Jacobs would put out when they carried the ball or went out for a pass, but they weren't going to block or tackle—for the team or State or Ralston or anyone else.

Chip kicked to the visitors' forty-yard line and the defensive platoon held Templeton for no gain. The game developed into a kicking contest until there were four minutes left to play in the second quarter. State had the ball on their own forty-yard line and Chip threw five consecutive passes.

The Statesmen had moved to the Templeton eighteen-yard line through the air. On second down, four to go, Chip passed to Montague. The slender end pulled in the ball but two of the Templeton players hit him so hard that he fumbled and the visitors recovered. With less than a minute to play, Templeton held on to the ball and two plays later the period ended. The score at the half: Templeton 7, State 0.

State controlled the ball through the third quarter but couldn't score. In the last quarter, with State in possession on their own forty-five-yard line, Ralston sent in all his veterans and Chip opened up.

Using his best sequence series, he sent Finley through the middle for six yards. Ace picked up three yards but his knee was injured on the play and he was carried from the field. Aker replaced him. When time was in, Speed cut through right tackle for five.

First and ten on the Templeton forty-one-yard line, now, and on the way back to the huddle, Chip figured the visitors were ripe for a trick pass. "Formation right! Double reverse pass! To Monty, to Whitty, and back to me! Keep going, Monty! On two! Hip!"

It was a difficult play but everything clicked. Chip faked to Fireball, then to Aker, and slipped the ball to Montague and faded back. Montague drove to the left and handed the ball to Whittemore. Whitty raced toward the right and then lateraled to Chip. He faked a pass to Speed and then saw Fireball swerve to the left in front of the goal. He aimed the ball for the corner of the end zone and Fireball pulled it in with a tremendous leap. State was back in the ball game!

A few seconds later Chip hit Whittemore with a basketball toss over the line for the two-point play and the Statesmen took the lead. The score: State 8, Templeton 7.

The State fans were deliriously happy. The lead had been a long time coming. Templeton chose to receive and sent in an entire new team. The visitors' coach had substituted freely all through the game, whereas Ralston had made only a few replacements. Now, he decided to give Morris and Montague a rest and replaced them with Jacobs and Schwartz. The Statesmen got a standing ovation as they trotted back to line up for the kick.

Chip groaned to himself when Eddie Aker came in to replace Speed. The touchdown twins again. One was bad enough! He glanced at the clock. Five minutes . . .

The visitors went to the air and advanced the ball to the fifty-yard line. State held, then, and Templeton kicked. Chip caught the ball on the State goal line and was downed on his own five. Three minutes to play!

Using the same repertory he had used at the start of the game, Chip sent Fireball barreling through the middle for five yards and then shifted right and used Aker for the cross buck for three. Now, if his strategy was right, Templeton would be expecting Jacobs on the wide reverse. He glanced at the clock. Forty seconds!

Back in the huddle he concentrated on Aker as he called the play. "Formation right! Nineteen keeper on two! I need a good fake, Aker! Let's go!"

On the "two" count Chip took Brennan's pass, pivoted to the right, and faked to Fireball. Then he clamped the ball on his thigh with his right hand and faked to Aker with his left. Fireball and Aker had covered up beautifully, and, still clutching the ball tightly against his thigh with his right hand, Chip slowed up and started his fake to Jacobs.

The Templeton forwards shifted toward the other side and the visitors' defense captain shouted: "Reverse! Watch the reverse!"

Chip's heart leaped. It had worked! He was away free! He shot a quick glance ahead. The visitors' end had dropped back a step and Soapy was just pulling out of the line and heading toward him. Then it happened!

Just as he finished the last fake and started his sprint, Jacobs made a grab for the hidden ball and it went spinning out of his hands, bobbing and bouncing back toward the State goal line. The why or wherefore was too much for Chip right then. All he knew was that the ball was gone and he was chasing it. "Ball!" he cried.

Chip was hit from the back and knocked from his feet by the Templeton left end. The big fellow dove for the ball, but he was too eager and his clutching fingers sent it spinning farther in the direction of the goal line. Then someone knocked the ball across the goal line and into the end zone and Chip groaned in dismay as a Templeton player fell on the elusive pigskin just as the timer's gun exploded ending the game.

The referee's arms shot over his head. Touchdown!

The fans on the visitors' side of the stadium were going wild as Chip got slowly to his feet, still trying to figure out why Jacobs had tried to grab the ball. It was fantastically unbelievable that the fellow had misunderstood the play. Then he heard Whitty's shout.

"I saw you!" Whittemore shouted angrily, charging toward Jacobs. "You grabbed that ball on purpose! You—you sneak!"

The umpire stepped between the two players but that didn't stop Whittemore. The big end was beyond reasoning. His face was livid with rage and he brushed the official aside as if he were a paper bag. Before anyone could stop him, Whittemore was on Jacobs, swinging with all his might. Chip ran toward Whitty and locked his arms. Biggie joined him a second later and it was all they could do to pull the infuriated giant away.

Then, just when Whittemore had partly calmed down, and while Chip and Biggie were still holding his arms, Eddie Aker smashed his right fist into Whittemore's mouth, cutting his lip and sending the blood flying. Soapy went into action with that, grabbed Aker from behind, wrestled him roughly to the ground, and sat on him. It was a mad, whirling, mixed-up skirmish and the Templeton players watched the debacle in amazement.

Coach Ralston, Rockwell, Sullivan, and half of the State players were out on the field, trying to help the angry officials.

"Take them out of the game," the referee cried. He pointed toward Whittemore, Aker, and Jacobs. "All of them! Out!"

Whittemore was raving again, trying to escape from the restraining arms of Chip and Biggie, intent on reaching Aker. But Sullivan and Rockwell grasped his arms and led him off the field. Ralston followed with Aker and Jacobs. A second later March, Gary Young, and Montague raced out and reported for the three banished players. Chip glanced at the bench and saw that Rockwell, Sullivan, and Murph Kelly were escorting Whitty, Aker, and Jacobs along the side line toward the player exit.

The angry referee plunked the ball down on the grass in front of the State goal. "Play ball!" he growled. "Line up for the try for the extra point."

Fighting mad, baffled, and frustrated, the demoralized Statesmen formed on the scrimmage line. But they rose up to stop an off-tackle smash. The game was over and Templeton had engineered the first big upset of the season. The final score: Templeton 13, State 8.

CHAPTER 15

POOR SPORTSMANSHIP

"WHAT HAPPENED?" Biggie asked, as the defeated Statesmen walked slowly from the field.

"I don't know," Chip said dully. "Jacobs must have gotten mixed up."

"Oh, sure!" Soapy said angrily. "He was mixed up, all right! Mixed up enough to spoil the play. He did it on purpose. Just like Whitty said. I saw him grab the ball. He wasn't mixed up."

"That's right," Gibbons added. "We saw it from the bench."

"Chip was specific enough about the play in the huddle," Brennan said. "He called the nineteen keeper play. Jacobs knew—"

"It was a gift!" Gibbons raged.

"On a platter!" Fireball growled.

"Yeah," Brennan added. "Served up by State's famous touchdown twins."

"Coach shoulda known better," O'Malley growled.

When he reached the dressing room, Chip dropped down on a bench between Soapy and Fireball and began slowly to take off his uniform. Across the way he could hear the shouts and cheers and joyful cele-

120

bration in the Templeton dressing room but there were no cheers or yells or good-natured gibes here. The Statesmen were down, disgruntled and discouraged.

He was pulling the tape from his ankles when Murph Kelly bellowed for silence. "Coach wants to say something—"

Ralston and Rockwell were waiting quietly in the center of the big room. "All right, fellows," the coach said in even tones, as he glanced from player to player. "It was a tough one to lose. We had some bad breaks today but we were beaten by a better team. My only satisfaction from the game is that you gave all you had and that's all anyone can ask.

"Fortunately, it was a nonconference game. It's hard to take a licking at any time. But I think it's more trying to get beaten the first game of the season at home, and in front of a fellow's friends and families, than at any other time. However, it's done and over and past and the sooner forgotten the better—

"It's a poor time to rehash the unpleasantness we witnessed this afternoon out on the field. In our own house, so to speak, before thirty thousand people who turned out to see a clean, hard game of football.

"In all my years of coaching I have never seen such a disgraceful display of poor sportsmanship, lack of emotional control, unrestrained actions, and contemptible disregard for the spirit of the game. So, the players who took part have been dismissed from the squad—

"Now, back to something a little more pleasant. One defeat does not make a season and I never felt it did a fellow any good to look over his shoulder and try to count his mistakes. I, for one, am looking ahead to the conference championship. I hope you are, too. A victory over Brandon next Saturday will be the first big step."

After Ralston and Rockwell left, Chip dressed slowly and then walked to State Drug with Soapy and Fireball. It was a long evening. Skip tried to cheer him up but his attempts merely added to Chip's gloom. The youngster had sat with his uncle and Coach Carpenter at the game and they had seen the disastrous fumble play.

"Uncle Merton was almost as mad as I was," Skip confided. "It's a good thing he didn't run into Mr. Jacobs or Mr. Aker at the game. He sure would have told them off. He said the touchdown twins come by their meanness legitimately enough; that the touchdown twins were just like their fathers when it came to poor sportsmanship."

Tech High School's football stadium was jammed with spectators. Chip was crowded in between Mr. Blaine and Sam Riggs, the pilot of the industrialist's private plane. They were seated on the fifty-yard line right behind the Tech bench by virtue of Skip's player passes. The Tech band was parading down the center of the field, led by its corps of girl baton twirlers, while the visitors' band was lined up behind the goal at the other end of the field. The players of both teams were warming up in front of their respective benches. Although it was not yet dark, the lights had been turned on and added to the colorful scene.

"Isn't it unusual for you and Skip both to be off on the same evening?" Blaine asked.

"Skip and I have been putting in extra time," Chip explained. "Besides, Mr. Grayson has extra week-end help."

"Get paid just the same?"

"Yes, sir."

"Grayson must be a football fan."

Chip smiled. "He is. He likes all sports."

"I can't understand why Skip wanted that job," Blaine mused, half to himself and half aloud. He turned and eyed Chip curiously. "Nor you, either," he said, "come to think of it. Don't you have an athletic scholarship? Doesn't it take care of all your expenses?"

"No, I don't, Mr. Blaine."

"You mean they didn't give you a scholarship? The way you can play football?"

"They offered me a scholarship but I prefer to work."

"What in the world for?"

Chip thought a moment before replying. Then he spoke slowly and carefully. "Well, for one thing, I have no scholarship obligations. I can play or quit and no one can complain."

"Don't you like football?"

"Oh, sure! I like a lot of things about football—the excitement and thrills of playing and being with the fellows and part of a team."

"You could have all that and still not have to work. I don't get it." He leaned forward and addressed his pilot. "What do you think about it, Riggs?"

"Oh," the pilot said slowly, "I don't know much about football. I guess there's a sort of prestige that goes with a boy getting a scholarship for playing the game. It means he's considered something special, I guess."

"What's wrong with that?" Blaine asked.

"Well," the pilot continued thoughtfully, "I guess

football is to Hilton what flying is to me. I fly because I love it. I guess Hilton plays football for sheer love of the game."

"What's that got to do with working?"

"Nothing," Riggs said. He pondered a moment and then continued, "Maybe Hilton likes to feel that he's playing football on his own. Frankly, if I could afford a plane I don't think I would work at flying."

Chip had listened to Riggs in admiration. The pilot's feelings about flying were the same as his own with respect to football.

"Well," Blaine concluded, "Skip won't have to worry about working or anything else. He's got a contract for four straight years at Brand. Board, room, tuition, books, fees, spending money—the works."

"I know," Chip said, nodding. "I saw it."

"You saw it?"

Chip nodded. "Yes. Skip showed it to me."

Blaine grinned. "I guess that's the reason he hasn't given it back. Must be showing it to everyone in town."

The parading was over out on the field and the teams had circled in front of their benches. The cheerleaders for both teams alternated in leading a cheer and the officials gathered in a little knot in the middle of the field. Chip felt a glow of pride when Skip dashed out from the Tech bench. The appearance of the All-State star set off a crowd cheer which was deafening. There was no question how the fans felt about Skip Miller.

The crowd quieted while the officials were meeting with the captains. Two men sitting directly in front of Mr. Blaine began talking about Skip. "He looks like Hilton," one man said. "Like State's All-America quarterback."

"You mean they didn't give you a scholarship?"

"Couldn't carry Hilton's shoes," the other said disdainfully.

"Well, he can carry one of them! And the way he's developing, he'll be able to carry 'em both in another year or so."

Blaine grinned and elbowed Chip. He was enjoying the conversation and leaned forward so he wouldn't miss any of it. Chip was embarrassed but he could do nothing about it.

"Wonder what the kid is going to do about college? I heard that more than a hundred coaches have been after him."

The first speaker snickered. "Don't mean a thing. His uncle wants him to go to some college out on the West Coast."

"So what?"

"So he goes to the college out on the West Coast."

"What's the uncle got to do with it?"

"He's a big shot. You know that big plant just outside University? Well, he just about owns it."

"So?"

"So the kid's father works for him and what the uncle tells the father to do—he does. The kid, too!"

"Maybe you're right," the other agreed. "But it seems a shame the kid can't go to school right here where he grew up, where everyone knows him and all—"

The roar of the crowd burst forth again when the teams ran out on the field for the opening kickoff and checked the conversation. Chip breathed a sigh of relief. He had been ill at ease just being in the company of E. Merton Blaine without having to listen to a couple of fans talk about Chip Hilton. He was glad that he would have to leave early to get ready for the midnight train which the team was taking to Brandon.

The teams were lined up and Skip was standing in front of the Tech goal line, a little in advance of the position Chip always took. He looked at the Tech bench and located Coach Carpenter standing on the side line, anxiously watching his team.

Then the ball was in the air. It was a short kick and didn't reach Skip. That was the only reason he wasn't in the play. After the ball was down, as soon as the Tech team formed on the thirty-yard line, he took charge personally. He carried for ten yards on a keeper; passed to his left end for eight; carried again for six; passed to his right end for fifteen, and the steam-rolling would have continued on for a touchdown if the opponents' captain hadn't gotten his breath and suddenly realized the ball was on his own thirty-one-yard line.

The time-out didn't change anything. Skip took up right where he had left off when time resumed and the game was only six minutes old when Tech scored the first touchdown and Skip kicked the extra point. The opponents received but couldn't gain and had to punt. Then Skip started all over again. That's the way the game went. It was all Skip and the half ended with Tech leading 21 to 0.

It was time for Chip to leave and he thanked Mr. Blaine and shook hands warmly with Sam Riggs. He wouldn't forget the little pilot for a long time. And, that night, before the drumming of the sleeper's wheels lulled him to sleep, he was thinking of Riggs' philosophy. He guessed there were people all over like that if a fellow could only have a chance to know them.

CHAPTER 16

SOPHOMORE SPOILERS

BRANDON STADIUM was almost filled when the Statesmen ran out on the field. And by the time they had finished warming up, every seat was taken. Coach Ralston and Murph Kelly watched every move Ace Gibbons made. Chip could tell they were deeply concerned about Ace's knee.

Chip won the toss and chose to receive. The ball went to Speed on the kickoff and the fleet halfback carried to mid-field, nearly got away. But he was hit hard and was limping when he got up. Chip pulled one of Speed's arms over his shoulder and tried to help the speedster walk it off.

"It's pretty bad, Chip. I don't think I can run on it."

Chip motioned toward the bench and Ralston sent Gary Young in to replace Speed. On the first play from scrimmage, Chip hit Montague with a bullet pass on the Brandon ten-yard line and the slender end scored standing up.

Brandon came right back and scored and the teams alternated touchdowns once more. It was 14 to 14 at the half, and 16 to 14 in favor of Brandon at the end of the third quarter. In the fourth quarter Chip inter-

cepted a Brandon pass and Ace Gibbons' key block
made it possible for him to go all the way for the
touchdown. Ace's block had been beautiful to see but
it had been costly. His knee had been hurt again and
Murph Kelly took him out of the game.

Coach Ralston sent Bob Horton in to replace Ace,
and Chip kicked the extra point to make the score:
State 21, Brandon 16.

Chip kicked off and the Statesmen's fighting defense backed up by his kicking held Brandon in their
own territory for the rest of the game. The final score:
State 21, Brandon 16.

It was a happy squad that piled on the nine-o'clock
train back to University. The Statesmen had won
their first conference game and the players were
looking ahead to the rest of the games, discussing the
strong and the weak teams in the conference.

Chip wasn't engaging in that foolishness. Every
game and every team was tough. He was thinking
about Ace and Speed. Murph Kelly had said Speed's
ankle was sprained and Ace's knee was about as bad.
"Seven more to go," he murmured, shaking his head
worriedly. Without Whitty and the touchdown
twins the future was far from bright.

The train reached University at nine o'clock Sunday morning and the platform was crowded with
friends and fans. Chip and Soapy helped Speed
down the steps of the car and the first person they
saw was Skip. Whittemore was right behind him.
Skip rushed forward and grabbed their bags. "Wel-
come home! Nice going! Nice run, Chip! Gee, Speed,
tough luck. Follow me, gang—"

Skip led the way to the end of the platform and
nodded toward a glittering Cadillac convertible
standing at the curb. "Not bad, eh?"

"Wow!" Soapy said. "What a dream boat!"

"Get in," Skip said, "I'll drive you out to Jeff."

"Your old man must be in the chips," Soapy said admiringly.

"It isn't his," Skip said. "It belongs to Uncle Merton."

"I thought so," Chip said. "The first thing you know, you'll be so obligated to your uncle that you'll *have* to go to Brand."

"No, I won't."

"What about the contract?"

"I haven't signed it and I'm not going to."

"Well," Soapy said impatiently, "let's get this jalopy rolling."

Whittemore sat beside Skip in the front seat and Chip and Soapy flanked Speed in the back and the powerful car rolled smoothly away. Whittemore passed a copy of the *Herald* back to Chip. "Look at the headline!" he said.

"Oh, no," Chip said shortly.

STATE'S ALL-AMERICA STARS AS FIREBRANDS BOW, 21–16

Brandon, Oct. 1 (AP)—Chip Hilton hit Chris Montague with a scoring pass on the first scrimmage play of the game here today and sprung the Statesmen to a 21–16 triumph over Brandon before a Firebrand Stadium throng of 32,290.

The Hilton-Montague passing combination enabled the Statesmen to match Brandon's two touchdowns until the second half when the Firebrands went two points ahead on a safety. Then Hilton brought the Statesmen from behind with a pass interception on the State 32-yard line and his 68-yard touchdown gallop iced the bitter struggle.

"Now look at Bill Bell's column," Whittemore said.

"I'll read it out loud," Soapy said. "Hey, listen to this!

" 'As predicted in this column yesterday, State's much-publicized touchdown twins, Eddie Aker and Jack Jacobs, did not make the trip to Brandon. The Sorry Sophomore Spoilers are being disciplined by Coach Curly Ralston for their part in the battle royal during the Templeton game. Judging from their performance in the Templeton game and the ease with which they committed so many disastrous mistakes, it is probably a good thing they were left behind.' "

Soapy paused and added a stertorous "Amen" and then continued:

" 'Ralston was back with his veterans yesterday and most of them played sixty minutes of football. Much was expected of State this year, but it is the opinion of this writer that Ralston's team will be lucky to squeak through the season without a few more injuries, and that means a few more defeats—despite the brilliance of Chip Hilton and State's great forward line.

" 'In fact, Ace Gibbons, last year's captain, is already handicapped with a sprained knee which forced him to the side line in the last quarter of the Brandon game and Speed Morris is nursing a sprained ankle which will side line him for at least a month. . . .' "

Chip reached over and took the paper out of Soapy's hands. Then, to the amazement of his two companions, he said: "That's why we need Aker and Jacobs."

Skip nearly ran the Cadillac up on the curb. "*Need* them?" he echoed. "Are you serious?"

"I was never more serious in my life," Chip said

grimly. "And I intend to get them back. Whitty, too!"

"Aw, Chip," Soapy protested, "come off it. Aker and Jacobs aren't worth it. Whitty, yes. Aker and Jacobs, no."

"Amen," Speed said, imitating Soapy.

"It's got to be all three or none," Chip said.

"You're wasting your time," Whittemore said, shaking his head.

"Not if you're willing to help."

"What can I do?"

"Apologize to Jacobs."

The big end leaned back over the seat and looked at Chip in astonishment. "You mean you want me to apologize?"

"That's right."

"You're kidding. Why should I apologize?"

"You started the trouble. You hit him first."

"But I saw him deliberately grab the ball."

"Perhaps you did," Chip said. "But that didn't give you the right to hit him."

Whittemore shook his head. "I still don't get it."

"You want to play football, don't you? You surely want to help the team."

Whittemore nodded. "Of course."

"All right, then. You can make a big step toward getting back on the team by apologizing to Jacobs."

"How about Aker? How about him apologizing to me? He hit me first." Whittemore rubbed his mouth gently. "And last!" he added grimly.

"I think he will apologize to you if you talk to Jacobs."

Whittemore scratched his head and thought it over. "I tell you what," he said thoughtfully. "I'll let you know in a couple of days. O.K.?"

Skip pulled up in front of Jeff with a flourish and

Chip and Soapy helped Speed up to his room. Then they spent the rest of the day studying.

Whittemore's "couple of days" lasted all week. Chip mentioned it once or twice but the big end put him off. The big game with Eastern was the talk of the campus and the town and State Drug, and Chip was kept busy with Ralston's new plays and defensive plans for the game.

The *Herald* and the *News* played up the Eastern players and the national title ambitions of the visitors every day, but Chip and the rest of the veterans weren't impressed. Eastern was an independent team and a victory or a loss meant nothing in the conference standing. So Chip and the majority of his teammates were looking forward to the game, felt that it was a great opportunity for State to upset the favorite.

Ralston spent a lot of time with Eddie Anderson and Bob Horton during the week, breaking them in as halfbacks. But neither showed promise and it was obvious to the rest of the squad that Chip and Fireball would have to carry the burden of the offense all alone.

Chip practiced his passing with Red and Monty every evening. But neither could come close to replacing Whitty. Red wasn't as big and he didn't have the hands or the pass-receiving know-how. Monty was tall and fast, but he was frail and inconsistent. He was so slender that Chip winced every time the skinny sophomore was tackled or tried to throw a block.

Saturday dawned clear and cold with only a slight breeze. Chip, Soapy, and Fireball took a cab from State Drug at twelve o'clock and an hour later they were out on the field. Chip started slowly with his kicking, watching the Eastern kicker who was punting on the opposite side of the field, figuring the distance and height of his opponent's punts. Soon, they were matching booming punts.

While he was kicking, he was thinking ahead to the game. Ace was going to start, but Chip didn't think he would be much help. Ace's knee was bandaged until it was the size of a pillow. "I'll do a lot of passing and running myself," he breathed. "That will take the pressure off him. . . ."

He got his chance on the opening kickoff. He won the toss and chose to receive. The ball came straight to him on the State goal line. He headed upfield and made it to the twenty-five-yard line before he was gang-tackled and buried under a pile of bulky bodies. The piling-on seemed a little too vicious to Chip and it must have seemed the same to the referee. After he had pulled the reluctant Eastern players off the pile, he glanced sharply at Chip and then picked up the ball and stepped off fifteen yards. "Piling on!" he growled, when the Eastern captain protested. "Play football."

Chip followed his plan, alternating his running and passing and State advanced to the Eastern twenty-seven-yard line before the drive was checked. Then, on fourth down, Chip booted a three-pointer and State was out in front.

The three points looked big during the first half. But the Statesmen were outmanned and the visitors pushed them down the field again and again. Eastern seemed to be knocking at the State door the entire thirty minutes. Chip ran and passed when he could and his long, perfectly placed punts held the opponents in check. The score at the end of the half: State 3, Eastern 0.

Eastern continued the same tactics in the second half; confined their attack to the ground; shuttled

their teams in and out in relays and kept the Statesmen on the defense. Eddie Anderson was trying but
lacked confidence. Ace couldn't run fast enough to do
any good, so it was Fireball on the short inside
plunges and Chip on the off-tackle slants and outside
sprints that kept State in the ball game. Eastern
would drive to the State twenty and then run into a
fighting defense which refused to give an inch.

Every State fan in the stadium was on his feet as
the game drew to a close, his support blending in with
the others and expressing the appreciation of all of
them in a continuous roar of approval. Eleven State
players outfighting three teams; holding one of the
football powers of the nation at bay. No! Beating
them! Leading in the score! This was a team!

With ten seconds to play, the ball on the State
thirty-yard line, third down and seven to go, Eastern
took a time-out. Ralston hadn't made a substitution.
Chip glanced at the dirty, sweat-soaked uniforms and
the drawn, tired faces of his teammates and his heart
swelled with pride. Ace was a battered wreck of a
man, hardly able to move. Monty was all in but still
game. Eddie Anderson was ready to drop. Chip
looked at the clock. Ten seconds. If they could only
hold once more. . . .

An entire Eastern platoon came racing in; uniforms
new, shiny, clean, and dry; confident in action and
manner, spirits high.

"Only ten more seconds, gang," Chip said. "One
more play."

Time was in, now, and Eastern came charging out
of their huddle and formed in the same tight, power-
packed formation. The play started off like a sweep,
but it was a fake, and the quarterback faded back for
a pass. Two receivers were splitting Ace in his defen-

sive right-halfback position and a fleet halfback was sprinting toward Chip.

He saw the play coming. The Eastern quarterback had known about Ace's knee all along.

It was a reckless move, but Chip left his position, sprinted for all he was worth to help Ace. But even as he raced toward the fighting halfback, he knew it was too late. The visitors' quarterback dug in and fired a perfect peg to the outside receiver and the end caught the ball without breaking stride. The other receiver took Ace out an instant later with a hard block and the ball carrier crossed the goal ten feet ahead of Chip. Touchdown!

Chip hurried back to help Ace to his feet but the veteran halfback couldn't make it. He rested painfully on his good knee, shaking his head in remorse. "I'm sorry about the pass, Chip," he said. "My knee just seemed to give out."

Murph Kelly came in with two of his assistants and they put Ace's arms over their shoulders and led him from the field. Gary Young reported for Ace and the teams formed for the extra point. The Eastern kicker booted a perfect placement and the game was over. The score: Eastern 7, State 3.

Most of the visiting scouts had taken copious notes covering the offensive and defensive formations used by the Statesmen. But the keen-eyed A. & M. scout had written only a few significant sentences. "Eleven players. No reserves. Injuries. A triple-threat quarterback who can do everything but who has only a fullback to run the ball and no pass receivers. Number 22, bad leg. Flood his zone with passes. Make State play a sixty-minute game; tire them out."

CHAPTER 17

A LOT OF HEART

WHITTEMORE glanced at Skip and tossed the sports page of the *Herald* on the desk. "Did you see what Bill Bell said about the team?"

"I saw it," Skip said quickly. "He said State was a team with a lot of handicaps but a team with a lot of heart."

"That's right," Whittemore said soberly. "It made me feel like two cents. When can we go see Jack Jacobs?"

Chip was caught by surprise. But only for a second. "You mean it?"

"I sure do!" Whittemore said firmly. "The sooner the better."

"I know where they hang out," Skip said eagerly. "Joe's Restaurant. Want me to see if they're there?"

Chip thought about it for a few seconds. "It's only two blocks," he said tentatively.

"I'll be right back," Skip said, dashing for the door.

It seemed as if Skip had been gone only two minutes before he was back, breathing rapidly. "They're there!" he said breathlessly. "Just the two of them. Studying! In the last booth on the right."

"Let's go!" Whittemore said shortly.

There were only a few customers in Joe's Restaurant. Just as Skip had said, Eddie Aker and Jack Jacobs were seated in the last booth, their books and papers spread out on the table.

Chip and Whitty stopped beside the booth and Eddie Aker looked up in surprise. His expression changed instantly to wariness as he nudged Jacobs. "Look who's here! Surprise, surprise!"

"Mind if we sit down?" Chip asked.

"Mind?" Jacobs said elaborately. "Why, we're delighted!" He winked at Aker and waved toward the other side of the table. "Sit down. Imagine meeting the famous All-America passing combination face to face."

"We've met before," Chip said calmly.

"What's on *your* mind?" Jacobs asked, looking at Whittemore.

"Something you probably least expect," Whittemore said. "Anyway, I'm here to apologize for starting the trouble on the field. I'm sorry. That good enough?"

Jacobs' jaw slacked and he gazed at Whittemore in surprise. "Why—why I guess so," he managed. "What happened to you?"

"I don't suppose you read Bill Bell's column today, did you?"

Jacobs shook his head. "I never read Bill Bell's column. What was so important about it?"

Whittemore pulled a clipping out of his pocket and smoothed it out on the table between Jacobs and Aker. "Read it," he said quietly.

Jacobs and Aker read the clipping clear through to the end. Then Aker looked up and smiled. "I get it," he said, grinning maliciously. "You want to patch things up and then go crawling back to Ralston and tell him you apologized and you're sorry and he'll put you back on the team. Right?"

"Sure!" Jacobs said. "That's it! Hilton needs his favorite pass receiver."

"The *team* needs him," Chip said gently. "And the team needs you fellows. Badly."

"Sure!" Aker said bitterly. "Sure the team needs us. Now that your pals are hurt."

"Ralston send you?" Jacobs asked.

Chip shook his head. "No one sent us. Whitty and I figured if we could get the trouble with you fellows straightened out, the coach might forget about it."

"We're not interested," Aker said coldly. "We're going to transfer out of State. Pop and Jack's father are trying to get us into Brand. They know the head of the Brand Athletic Association."

"That's right," Jacobs added. "We couldn't care less about Ralston or State or—"

"Or you two guys," Aker added. "Wait!" he said quickly. "I'll take that back. I guess *you're* all right. It's the rest of that bunch. I'm sorry I hit you, Whittemore."

"I'm glad you said that Aker," Chip said.

"Me, too," Whittemore added.

"I guess you fellows understand about the transfer rule," Chip said. "You'll have to sit out a year, lose a whole season of football."

"So what!" Jacobs said carelessly, shrugging his shoulders.

Chip felt that he had made progress and he didn't want to push his luck. Now, if he could bring the team into line he would be in a good position to approach

Ralston. "Well," he said, rising from the table, "I have to get back to work. Sorry you fellows can't see it our way. Let's go, Whitty."

Skip was waiting when they got back to the stockroom. "What happened?" he asked.

Whitty told him about the conversation while he was putting on his fountain coat. "So," he concluded, "it looks as if we had a nice walk—"

"I know one thing," Skip said. "They won't get very far with Uncle Merton. He thinks they're the world's worst."

Chip hoped that Skip was right. If Mr. Blaine turned Aker and Jacobs down it would be a big help. But, no matter how Aker and Jacobs made out with Blaine, he sure wasn't going to give up. . . .

Coach Ralston called off all scrimmage for the week, giving his tired and injured regulars a rest. Ace and Speed managed to get loosened up by Friday afternoon, and when the Statesmen left for Southwestern that night they had high hopes that their two injured backfield stars would be all right for the second conference game of the season.

But the next afternoon Ace lasted only one play. Chip won the toss and chose to receive. The kick went to Fireball and he carried to the thirty-one-yard line.

Ace hobbled into the huddle, his face drawn with pain. "It's out again," he groaned. "Sorry, Chip, fellows, I can't do you any good."

Gary Young replaced Ace. And, once again, Chip found himself in the middle of a game with only Fireball to depend upon for ball-carrying help.

Southwestern stressed defense, and when the Statesmen failed to penetrate beyond the Southwestern twenty-yard line, Chip place-kicked for three points. The home team received and marched the length of the field, using a spread formation for short passes and end runs to score. They failed to kick the extra point. Chip kicked another placement in the second quarter and the score was tied at 6 to 6 when the half ended.

Southwestern received, couldn't gain, and kicked to Chip on the State thirty-five-yard line. Then, on the first play, Young was hit hard, fumbled, and Southwestern recovered. Thirty seconds later the Southwestern quarterback passed to his left end and Young wasn't big enough to knock the ball away. The tall end pulled in the ball and carried to the nineteen-yard line. Three plays later they went around their left end for a touchdown. This time they kicked the extra point to take the lead 13 to 6.

The teams seesawed back and forth in the last quarter until there were three minutes left to play. Chip's kicking had forced Southwestern back and back. Now, he took a low punt and raced back to the home team's thirty-three-yard line.

He hit Montague with a short pass, carried himself to the eight-yard line on a keeper play, and hit Montague in the end zone for the touchdown. Southwestern led by a single point, 13 to 12, and Chip faced a difficult decision. A successful place kick would tie the score; a successful running play or pass would win the game. *And* a failure on either play meant defeat. . . .

Chip looked at the tired faces of his teammates and grinned confidently. "We'll go for the two points! O.K.? All right! Keeper 9 X! On two! Let's win! Hip!"

The Southwestern fans were chanting, "Block that kick! Block that kick!" But when State broke for the line and formed in scrimmage formation, they changed to: "Hold that line! Hold that line!"

Chip faked to Fireball, to Young, and tore around right end with Soapy leading the way. The redhead dropped the outside line-backer and Chip ran clear to the side line before he cut in and plunged across the goal line for the two points.

The chant of the home fans ended in a groan as the referee raised his hands and the big numbers under the clock showed the score: Visitors 14, Southwestern 13.

There was time for one more play. Southwestern received and Chip booted a high kick and the ball carried to Southwestern's thirty-yard line. Biggie, Soapy, and Red hit the fullback an instant after he caught the ball and the game was over. State had bounced back into the winning column.

When the team pulled into University the next morning the platform was crowded with students and fans. Skip met Chip and Soapy just as he had after the Brandon game. But this time, to Soapy's disappointment, Skip wasn't driving the Cadillac.

"Where's the dream boat?" Soapy demanded.

"I'm not driving it any more," Skip said.

"Fine thing!" Soapy grumbled. "Why not?"

"I don't want to obligate myself," Skip said, winking at Chip. "Hey! Nice win, you guys. We won, too!"

"Chip won it," Soapy said.

"The papers say the same thing," Skip said, grinning. "This week the headline reads: 'Hilton Upsets Unbeaten Southwestern!'"

"Of all the nonsense—" Chip began.

"Oh, yes," Skip interrupted, "Western beat A. & M.!"

"No!" Soapy exploded.

"That's right!"

"Well, whaddaya know," Soapy said. He counted

on his fingers. "Now all we gotta do is beat Cathedral, Southern, Midwestern, Western, and A. & M.! Heck, it's a cinch! A. & M. beat Cathedral 87 to 6; we'll take Southern easy. Midwestern and Western are tough but we'll kill A. & M.—"

"If you don't run out of players," Skip said.

"Let's concentrate on Cathedral," Chip said, "and win—"

"I know, I know," Soapy interrupted. "And win 'em one at a time."

Cathedral fielded a fighting team and what had figured to be an easy victory turned into a bitter battle. Playing without Ace and Speed, State scored first, chiefly on Fireball's inside plunging and Chip's dashes off tackle and around the ends. Chip kicked the goal for the extra point. The visitors came right back, took the kickoff, and marched the length of the field to score and kick the goal for the extra point. Chip kicked two field goals in the second quarter and State led, 13 to 7, at the half.

The visitors went ahead in the third quarter to lead 15 to 13. But, with time running out in the last quarter, Chip faded back to pass. Cathedral had Montague covered like a blanket and Chip hit Fireball with a pass over the line following a fake plunge. The speedy blockbuster sprinted thirty yards for the touchdown. That put State out in front, 19 to 15. On the try after touchdown, Chip fooled Cathedral with a fake place kick and passed to Red in the end zone for the two points. The final score: State 21, Cathedral 15.

The victory ran State's conference record to three wins and no defeats but the problem of the halfback positions, offensively and defensively, was cause for alarm and dampened the team's enthusiasm. Coach Ralston worked feverishly all week but little progress seemed to have been made when the team entrained Friday afternoon for the game with Southern.

The game developed into another dogfight. The home team was big and determined and scored twice in the first half to State's once and led, 14 to 7, at the intermission. In the third quarter Southern kicked a placement to lead 17 to 7, but State came right back and scored on a long run by Chip and a thirty-yard pass, Chip to Finley for the touchdown. Chip passed to Montague for the extra points. That made the score: Southern 17, State 15.

After several punt exchanges toward the end of the fourth quarter, State wound up with the ball on the Southern thirty-two-yard line, fourth down, four to go, and time for just one more play. Chip debated with himself briefly and then called for a place kick.

Then, with the crowd roar rolling down on the field in a deafening bedlam of sounds, Chip toed the important kick of the game. With Young holding, he booted a three-point placement. The score: Southern 17, State 18.

The battle-weary Statesmen could hardly walk, but they weren't too tired to get Chip up on their shoulders and carry him all the way to the dressing room. "Four straight conference wins!" Soapy shouted gleefully. "And only three to go!"

CHAPTER 18

IN THE GRANDSTAND

CHIP AND SOAPY were reading the Sunday papers when someone bellowed up from Jeff's first floor. "Chip Hilton! Chip, someone out front to see you."

"Now who could that be?" Chip muttered. He walked over to the door. "Coming," he called. "Coming right down."

Soapy bounded to the window and looked down at the street. "It's the Cadillac Skip was driving," he said excitedly. "Top down and everything! There's a big man sitting in the back seat smoking a cigar. Must be Skip's uncle."

"I hope not," Chip said, slipping on his jacket. "I wonder what's up?"

A man in chauffeur's uniform was waiting on the porch. "Chip Hilton?" he asked. Without waiting for Chip's reply he gestured toward the street. "Mr. Blaine would like to speak to you."

Blaine took a last puff from his cigar and tossed it away when Chip approached. "Hello, Hilton. Glad you were home. How about a little drive?"

"All right, Mr. Blaine," Chip said reluctantly.

The chauffeur held the car door open and Chip sat down beside Mr. Blaine. As the car rolled smoothly away, Chip glanced up at the window of his room on the second floor. Soapy was leaning far out of the window, waving good-by.

"Oh, before I forget it," Mr. Blaine said. "How did you make out with the touchdown twins?"

Chip glanced at the big man in surprise. "How did—"

Blaine smiled. "Skip keeps me pretty well advised with respect to your activities."

Chip shook his head ruefully. "I'm not doing too well, I guess."

"From what Skip said, they were counting on transferring to Brand."

"I know," Chip said, nodding.

"Well," Blaine continued, "the two boys and their fathers paid me a little visit a day or two ago. They had a lot of misconceptions concerning the Brand recruiting methods for one thing, and they were all mixed up with respect to the kind of athletes we want. I think I straightened them out on both counts.

"We wouldn't have them at Brand. They wouldn't last five minutes with Stew Peterson, and unless I'm greatly mistaken, they're not worth five minutes of *your* time."

"They've got a lot of ability," Chip said tentatively.

"Physically, yes," Blaine agreed. "But when it comes to guts, determination, and a knowledge of team play they haven't got a thing. And their fathers are just as bad. I told them so."

"But we haven't got any reserves, Mr. Blaine," Chip said. "Right now, we're using a guard and an end in the backfield."

"I know," Blaine said sympathetically. "I don't know where in the world you fellows mustered enough reserves to win any games, much less four."

He appraised Chip and continued, "From the looks of you, I would say that right now you need a long rest. Ralston is playing you too much. When a boy gets tired and fed up he goes stale. And that's when he gets hurt."

"There isn't much Coach Ralston can do about that," Chip said apologetically. "We're all playing sixty minutes. All the veterans, that is—"

Blaine nodded. "I know. But I'm getting away from the purpose of this little ride. I wanted to talk to you about Skip."

"About going to college?"

"That's right. The boy has gained a lot of confidence and independence since he got the job with you. He doesn't want to use my car and won't commit himself on Brand." Blaine paused and studied Chip before continuing. "Skip tells me you think he should go to State."

"I guess that's right," Chip said, nodding. "My father went to State, Mr. Blaine. But that isn't the only reason I came to school here. I was born in this state and I have always felt an athlete owed something to his home state. I'm for State first, last, and all the time."

There was a short, awkward pause as the powerful car moved swiftly along the open highway. Then Blaine resumed. "You know, Hilton, Skip's father has had rather tough sledding. Besides, he's an independent sort of a fellow. Now, when Skip needs his help, he is in no position to give any. In fact, he needs Skip's help."

"I thought Mr. Miller was working for you."

Blaine smiled. "Well, let's say he's working in one of my plants. In fact, the job he holds right now is a *made* job."

Chip wished he had never come on this ride. "Why in the world did I ever let myself get involved in Skip's problem?" he asked himself.

"You could help Skip a lot," Blaine continued. "His father knows he could really *earn* his pay in my western plant. He would go in a second if Skip went along."

"You want me to advise Skip to go to Brand," Chip said. "Isn't that right?"

"That's right," Blaine said. "It's best for everyone."

"I'm sorry, Mr. Blaine," Chip said firmly. "I can't do that." He faced the big man and looked him straight in the eyes. "I still think Skip should go to State. However, I assure you that I won't try to influence him. Skip should make his own decisions. If you don't mind, I'd like to go back."

"Sure, Hilton," Blaine said kindly. "We'll go back. I hope you won't say anything about this afternoon to Skip."

"I won't, Mr. Blaine."

The trip back was quiet and swift and Chip was glad when the car glided gently to a stop in front of Jeff. He thanked Mr. Blaine for the ride and got quickly out of the car, glad the ordeal was over, anxious to get back to his books.

Soapy had gone out somewhere and Chip spent the rest of the afternoon studying. Once in a while he took a break to think about Aker and Jacobs. Now that Mr. Blaine had turned them down on a transfer to Brand, maybe they would be more inclined to consider his plan. "I'll see them the first thing in the morning," he resolved.

His Monday schedule was light and Chip usually spent a lot of time studying in the library. But today he tramped about the campus looking for Aker and

Jacobs. It was noon before he caught up with them in the student union. They were sitting alone in one of the lounges, books piled on a table.

"Hiya, fellows," he said, dropping down into a chair beside them. "I've been looking for you. How's it going?"

"Better than it is with you," Jacobs said. "You look like a wreck. You must have lost fifteen pounds."

"Not quite," Chip said, smiling. "But I am a little tired."

"You ought to be," Aker said. "Ralston's been playing you every minute of the games."

"There isn't much else he can do, Eddie. That's why I'm here."

"I thought so," Jacobs said quickly. "Don't you *ever* give up?"

"Nope, I don't."

"You might as well," Aker said. "We're not going to knuckle down just to help Ralston out of a hole he dug himself."

"I'm not thinking about the coach," Chip said evenly. "It's the team. We need help."

"You don't need *us*," Aker said bitterly. "We've run into Gibbons and Brennan and some of the rest of them a dozen times and they treat us like we're dirt."

"And they've got half the campus acting the same way," Jacobs added.

"What do you expect?" Chip asked. "They think you quit."

"We didn't quit," Jacobs said sullenly. "Ralston *threw* us off the team. What would *you* do?"

"Try to get back," Chip said simply.

"Look, Hilton," Aker said, getting to his feet and gathering up his books, "we wanted to play football. That's why we came to State. But it wasn't any secret about how Gibbons and Brennan and the rest of the regulars felt about us. We got a little publicity and they ganged up on us from the very first day of camp. We *had* to fight back."

"Right!" Jacobs added. "Maybe we did get a little out of line, but we weren't going to knuckle down to them just because we were sophomores."

"We know we're not the greatest," Aker said. "But we know we're good enough to play varsity. And if those guys had been real guys we would have shown them we could block and tackle as well as they could. Nope!" he said, turning away, "they wanted to get rid of us, so we'll do our playing in the grandstand."

The two sophomores walked slowly away and Chip could scarcely conceal his jubilation. "They're coming around," he whispered. "Now to line up the team."

He approached Soapy, Biggie, Speed, Red, and Fireball first and had no difficulty in gaining their support. Then, on Wednesday, just before practice, he called a meeting of the starters and told them about his plan to get Whitty, Aker, and Jacobs back on the squad.

"Whitty, yes!" Brennan said. "The other two, no!"

"Right!" Joe Maxim agreed. "We want no part of *them.*"

"Let it ride until after the Midwestern game, Chip," Biggie advised.

"Let it ride, period!" Brennan growled. "We've made it this far. We don't need any help *now.*"

Saturday's game proved Mike Brennan's remark to be the understatement of the year. Midwestern was a strong defensive team and had State well scouted; they were ready for Finley's inside plunges and Chip's off-tackle slants and end runs. Double-teaming Montague, they throttled Chip's passes all through the first quarter.

In the second quarter, with the ball in the possession of the Statesmen on their own forty-five-yard line, second down and eight to go, Chip called for a delayed pass to Red. He faked to Finley, to Anderson, and dropped back for the throw. Then it happened!

Midwestern's right tackle and end rushed him and knocked him to the ground just as he released the ball. Chip was caught off balance and tried to break the fall with his right hand. He saw Red catch the ball just as his right hand hit the ground. Then the charging opponents fell heavily on top of him and his right arm was doubled under and behind his back.

Chip felt a tremendous pull and wrench in his shoulder and it hurt him so badly that he couldn't restrain a cry of pain. One of the opponents grasped him under the right arm to help him to his feet but Chip pushed him away with his good left arm. "Hold it," he said, getting slowly to his feet, his right arm hanging loosely at his side. "Oh, boy!"

Red had been tackled on the Midwestern thirty-second-yard line and he came tearing back to join the Statesmen who gathered around Chip. The exultant shout with which the State fans had greeted Red's catch died away as Murph Kelly ran out on the field. And the fans remained silent as Kelly led Chip from the field, shocked by the realization that the trainer had applied a hastily adjusted sling to the famous quarterback's throwing arm.

Ralston and Rockwell met them halfway to the bench, their faces etched with fear and concern. "How do you feel, Chip? What is it, Murph? Is it bad?"

"It's bad," Kelly said.

Doc Terring joined them as they moved along the side line and the fans rose to their feet and applauded Chip all the way to the players' exit. When they reached the dressing room, Doc Terring waited quietly as Kelly cut the jersey and the laces of the shoulder pads. Then, pressing gently on the shoulder, he examined it carefully. At the end, he breathed a sigh of relief and nodded reassuringly at Chip.

"I can't find any signs of a break, Chip. Just the same, we'll go up to the hospital for an X ray. You get dressed and I'll be right back. I want to talk to the coach."

Chip felt a tremendous pull in his shoulder

"It doesn't feel so bad now, Doc. You don't think I should go back?"

"Back?" Terring repeated. "Of course not! You dress."

While Kelly helped him off with his uniform, Chip tried to move his arm. But stiffness had set in and a dull pain began coursing through his shoulder. "Just like Mr. Blaine said," he breathed. "I *was* tired. Of all the times to get hurt . . ."

and he couldn't restrain a cry of pain

CHAPTER 19

FORGET THE PAST

THE SPORTS PAGE of Sunday's *Herald* lying open on the hospital bed told the story. Chip was sitting beside the window watching the driveway for Doc Terring's car and Soapy was sprawled on a chair in the corner staring glumly at the ceiling. The headlines kept running through Chip's thoughts: *State loses to Midwestern 7 to 0 for first conference loss. Chip Hilton hospitalized with shoulder injury. . . .*

"Here he comes," Chip said, leaping to his feet.

A few moments later Doc Terring knocked on the door and entered. He smiled at Soapy and turned to Chip. "Well, now," he said, "I expected to find you in bed."

"No, Doc, I'm all right. I feel fine. How about the X ray?"

Terring opened the envelope he was carrying and pulled out several prints. "Here they are. And not a sign of a break. Sit down on the side of the bed there and let's have a look." He took a long time examining the shoulder, nodding now and then but saying nothing.

Soapy couldn't stand the suspense. "How about it, Doc?"

"So, so," Terring said.

"How about getting out of here?" Chip asked.

"I guess so," Terring said. "I think I can immobilize your shoulder with some tape and a sling."

"How soon can I go out to practice?" Chip asked. "How long before I can start throwing?"

Terring shook his head. "You're not going to do any more throwing this year, Chip. You might as well get that through your head now as later."

"But I can still play, Doc. I don't have to throw. We have an open date next Saturday. That means I've got two weeks—"

"You mean play with one arm?"

"Sure, Doc. It's been done before."

"I know that," Terring said shortly. "Now, I want you to report to my office every afternoon. And until I give you a green light, you wear a sling. Now, as soon as I can check you out of here, I'll drive you home."

Terring dropped Chip and Soapy off at Jeff and all of their pals were waiting. The reception warmed Chip's heart; all of them were trying to conceal their feelings in solicitude and worry about his shoulder but underneath he knew they were discouraged.

It was the same the next day on the campus. The Midwestern defeat had tied up the conference leadership in a three-way tie between State, A. & M., and Western. But few State fans gave the injury-ridden Statesmen a ghost of a chance for the conference title. Especially with Chip on the list of invalids.

Doc Terring and Murph Kelly worked on his shoulder Monday afternoon and Chip watched practice from the side line. Much of the pain had disappeared from his shoulder, but he could barely lift his arm and he knew that Doc Terring was right. He wasn't going to be able to throw for a long time.

Skip was a tremendous help in the stockroom, taking hold to such an extent that Chip spent most of his time at the desk. Skip and his teammates were undefeated and the youngster should have been on top of the world. But he was upset by his uncle's persistent campaign to send him to Brand University and his spirits were low.

It seemed to Chip that he was surrounded by trouble and discouragement but that none of it made sense. Skip had only to take a determined stand and his uncle would come around. Blood was a lot thicker than water and the happiness of a fellow like Skip would certainly be more important to his uncle than the selection of a college just to play football. And, so far as the Statesmen were concerned, they were still tied for first place in the conference. In fact, they were a game ahead because they had played five conference games while Western and A. & M., had only played four. Further, anything could happen in football. . . .

Tuesday afternoon, Chip saw Doc Terring early and waited in the dressing room for the rest of his teammates. They were concerned about his shoulder but he had no time for that. "Never mind me," he said. "I'll be all right. What about Aker and Jacobs? You said we should wait until after the Midwestern game—"

There was an awkward silence. Then Mike Brennan cleared his throat and looked around as if for support. "How do we know they could help us, Chip? They never showed a thing."

"Perhaps that was partly our fault," Chip said. "At least they feel that way."

"*They* would!" Ace Gibbons said.

"It doesn't seem to me," Biggie said slowly, "that we're in a position to debate their ability. Holy socks! Ace is out with a bum knee, Speed's ankle is no better, and Chip—"

"I'll be able to play," Chip interrupted. "Well, what do you say?"

"I say we let Chip try to get 'em back," Fireball said. "We sure know Whitty can help and as far as Aker and Jacobs are concerned—what have we got to lose?"

"Nothing!" Soapy growled. "I'm game if they can help."

"They can help," Chip said. "But—"

"But what?" Brennan demanded.

"But isn't it important to think that we might help them? Help Aker and Jacobs? Why wouldn't it be a good idea to forget the past and give them a hand?"

"Nothing wrong with that," Maxim agreed.

There was a short silence. Then Mike Brennan shrugged his broad shoulders. "All right, Chip. Count us in. You can tell 'em we'll start all over. Clean!"

It took Chip three days to find Aker and Jacobs. They were always a little ahead or had come along after he had left. But on Friday he found them at lunch in the student union snack bar. Their attitude surprised him.

"How's your shoulder?" Aker asked.

"Coming along," Chip said, sitting down beside Jacobs. "Doc Terring says I can take the sling off this afternoon."

"You going to try to play?" Jacobs asked curiously.

"I sure am!"

"But I read in the paper that you wouldn't be able to throw," Aker observed.

"I can play without throwing. I was wondering about you fellows—"

"You know how we stand," Jacobs said uncertainly. "What about the other guys on the team?"

"They feel the same way I do," Chip said quickly.

"At least that's what they say," Aker said.

"How did you find *that* out?"

"Oh, we've still got a couple of friends on the team. They told us about the meeting you called last Tuesday and what you said."

"And the one you had with them before the Midwestern game, too," Jacobs added. "Er, I had you all wrong, Chip. I'm sorry about that."

"That goes for both of us," Aker said. "Now, about coming back—we're out a year of football any way you look at it. We might as well play if Ralston will give us a chance."

"That's right," Jacobs agreed. "But we want to do something else! We want to show Ralston and the guys on the team that we're *real* football players."

"It appears to me we're overlooking something," Aker said. "How about Ralston?"

"That's the next step," Chip said, rising to his feet. "Say, where can I reach you fellows?"

"We live at Davis Hall," Jacobs said, grinning. "Two blocks from Jeff."

"And we eat dinner at Joe's Restaurant every night," Aker added.

"Maybe we can change that to the training table," Chip said. "Starting Monday."

"Knowing Ralston as *we* do," Aker said, laughing, "I doubt it. Anyway, good luck."

That afternoon, Chip could hardly sit through his

last class. When it ended, he hurried across the campus to the field house and up the back stairs to the coaches' office. Henry Rockwell was working on some scouting notes when Chip knocked on the door but he pushed them aside.

"Hello, Chip. Come in. You look as if you've got something important on your mind."

"I have. Whittemore and Aker and Jacobs."

"Oh, that again. Let's hear it."

Chip told Rockwell about the progress he had made, about Whittemore's apology, the reaction of Aker and Jacobs, and the feeling of the members of the team. When he concluded, Rockwell nodded approvingly.

"You *have* been working. Now what?"

"That's what I wanted to ask you. I *had* planned to talk to the Dean—"

Rockwell shook his head vigorously. "Oh, no, Chip. That would stir the whole thing up again."

"What should I do?"

"Go see Coach Ralston. And there's no time like the present. He's in his office right now."

Chip took a deep breath. "All right," he said, "here goes!"

He found Ralston sitting with his back to his desk, staring moodily out the window. The coach was so absorbed in his thoughts that he didn't hear the knock on the door and Chip waited quietly. Then Ralston whirled his chair around and started in surprise when he saw Chip.

"Oh, hello, Hilton. How long have you been standing there?" He waved toward a chair. "Come in—sit down."

Ralston studied Chip for a moment. "Now don't tell me you want to come out to practice?"

"That's right," Chip said. "Doc Terring said I could come out Monday and do some running. In fact, he said I might be able to play a little against Western."

"With *that* shoulder? Uh, uh!"

"But Murph Kelly said he could put a shock cast on it. He said you could hit one of those with an ax and it wouldn't hurt."

"That's probably true. How about throwing?"

"I guess I won't be able to throw any more this year."

"Could you handle the ball?"

"Sure, Coach. Look!" Chip got to his feet and used his hands to fake imaginary hand-offs.

Ralston nodded. "That would help. But don't get your hopes up. You are still ex-athletics until you get Doc Terring's O.K. In writing!"

Chip was halfway to the door before he remembered the chief purpose of his visit. He turned back toward the desk. "I wanted to talk to you about something else, Coach. About Whittemore, Aker, and Jacobs."

The frown lines between Ralston's eyes deepened and his jaw firmed. "What about them?" he asked sharply.

"Well, Coach, they've apologized to one another and they want another chance. We— Well, the rest of the players and I would like to help them."

"Help them?"

"Yes, sir. The team needs help, but we feel that they need help, too."

Ralston turned his chair slowly around so that he faced the window. After a long silence he spoke over his shoulder. "You're right about helping Whittemore and the touchdown twins. They can come back, but I want it clearly understood that they are not being given another chance just to help us win games. Is that clear?"

"Yes, *sir*," Chip said, turning away. "Yes, *sir*."

Chip went into action as soon as he left Ralston's office. He hurried back to State Drug where he found Whittemore behind the fountain.

"Good news, Whitty," he cried. "Coach said to report to practice Monday. How about that?"

"You're kidding!"

"Not a chance."

Whittemore's "Yippee!" startled the customers at the fountain. Then he sobered. "How about Aker and Jacobs?"

"Same thing. I'm on my way to tell them now. Be back in twenty minutes."

Aker and Jacobs were as surprised as Whittemore had been, but they were also a bit nervous. "I don't know how you did it," Jacobs said. "You mean we don't have to do any more apologizing?"

"Nope."

Aker sighed in relief. "I'll never understand it."

"Me either," Jacobs added. "Look, Hilton—"

"The name is Chip."

Jacobs grinned. "All right, Chip. I— Well, we appreciate it."

"And you won't be sorry," Aker added.

Chip nodded and extended his hand. "I know that —Eddie, Jack."

CHAPTER **20**

CROSSED SIGNALS

THE STADIUM CLOCK showed four minutes left to play in the third quarter with Western leading 9 to 0. The Statesmen had the ball on their own thirty-yard line, third down, five yards to go. Chip checked the Western defense and groaned. The visitors were using the same tight 5-3-3 defense they had used all through the game, secure in the knowledge that Gary Young didn't have the arm to throw the long pass. It was really an eight-man line designed to stop Fireball's line smashes and to throttle Young's short passes.

"It's no good," Chip murmured, glancing along the bench. Whitty, Aker, and Jacobs were ready and waiting, watching Ralston with eager eyes. With Aker and Jacobs to throw from the right or left and Fireball from the deep position, Western would have been forced to change their alignment. And with Whitty to sprint deep into their pass defense, they would have been forced to back up, worry about their secondary defense. But just as it had been in practice all week, Ralston acted as if he didn't know they were on the field.

Ralston had used Chip twice in the first half, once to handle the ball and direct the attack, and once to kick out of a hole from the State two-yard line. When Chip had handled the ball, Western had used a close 6–3–2 defense, virtually a nine-man line. His shoulder injury was known to every scout and team in the conference. Chip had counted on that; had thought about it all week.

He glanced at the scoreboard and shook his head. His secret surprise would be good for only one play. The way it stood right now, one touchdown would not be enough. . . .

Fireball punted the ball down to the Western eighteen-yard line, the ball drilling through the air in a low, flat trajectory like a bullet. The visitors' safety man backed up, noting that the Statesmen covering the kick were far behind the ball. Right then, the pigskin was nosing down and he made the mistake of taking one last look. The ball was just above his head when he looked up and it hit him in the chest and slipped through his frantic grasp and bounded back toward the wave of oncoming Statesmen. He dashed forward as Biggie dove for the ball. A second later the referee blasted his whistle and pointed toward the Western goal.

State's ball!

It was first and ten on Western's twenty-two-yard line, and after Fireball plunged for three yards through the line and Young's pass into the flat was incomplete, Ralston bellowed for Chip.

"Hilton! Quick! For Horton! Take Morris with you —for Anderson. Use a keeper play to get into position and then kick!"

Chip and Speed reported and then dropped into the huddle. "All right, gang!" Chip said. "I've got to get in position for a kick! Keeper to the right on three!"

He carried for a yard, but the down placed the ball twenty yards in on the Western eighteen-yard line. They hurried out of the huddle and Speed knelt six yards back of Brennan and handled the pass beautifully, catching and setting the ball down in one motion a split second before Chip booted it between the uprights. He could have kicked that one blindfolded.

The score: Western 9, State 3.

The quarter had ended on the last play and the teams changed goals. Horton and Anderson came racing in to replace Chip and Speed, and they trotted off the field with the cheers of the State fans riding with them all the way. Chip breathed a deep sigh of relief as he dropped down on the bench. The stage was set. . . .

During the next ten minutes, Ralston sent Chip in twice to kick the Statesmen out of trouble and his booming punts held Western even. On the last punt, Ralston left him in the game. Western played it smart and passed into his zone, a long, high spiral which appeared to be going over his head and into the hands of their speeding left end. But, at the last second, Chip leaped high in the air and pulled the ball in with his left hand. He pivoted around but the end was right behind him and dropped him on the twenty-five-yard line.

Western was still in their tight 6–3–2 defense, concentrated on stopping the running of Chip and Fireball. State was held for a scant five yards in three downs and it was fourth down on the State thirty-yard line. Chip's heart was pounding. It was now or never. . . .

Western took a time-out and Gary Young came trotting in to replace him with orders for Fireball to punt. But Chip refused the substitution, and sent Young

back to the bench. He moved wearily over beside
Schwartz and knelt to tighten the lace of his kicking
shoe. "Red!" he whispered sibilantly. "Forget all
about the receiver—"

"Do what?"

"Be quiet and listen! Never mind what I say in the
huddle—just run! Run for the left corner of the end
zone! Get it?"

The referee's whistle shrilled and Chip turned abruptly away from Red and took his position in the
huddle. He glanced at the scoreboard. Two minutes
to play. . . .

The State fans groaned when the Statesmen
formed in kick formation and the Western rooters began to chant the familiar: "Block that kick! Block that
kick!"

The ball spiraled back and, extending the ball at
arm's length, Chip took his rocker and stepped forward, concentrating on the ball. Red and Biggie and
Brennan and Montague were streaking up the field
toward the Western safety man and his heart leaped
when he saw the Western right end slant sharply in
toward him.

Then, just as the visitors' forwards broke through
the kicking pocket, Chip pivoted and cut out to the
left, running for his life. The charging Westerners
checked their rush and chased him as their right line-
backer raced out to make the tackle.

Far up the field, Red cast a frantic glance over his
shoulder and angled for the side line. At the same
time, the Western safety man saw Red's move and
Chip running to the left. "Pass!" he yelled. "Pass!"

Chip waited no longer, stabbed his left foot in the
ground, and made a left-handed pass, threw the ball
with all his might; with all the strength of his left

arm. It was a mighty heave and he felt the sharp protest of the unused throwing muscles of his left arm just as the Western line-backer knocked him to the ground. The roar from the stands told him all he wanted to know, but he scrambled to his knees just in time to see Red cross the goal line.

Touchdown!

Pandemonium in the stands! Teammates gone mad on the field! A miracle!

Fireball and Soapy raced over and lifted him to his feet, and practically carried him up the field. Both were yelling something about fake punts and crossed signals and secret plays, but the roar of the crowd drowned out all the sense of their words and it didn't make any difference what they were saying, anyway.

Chip's eyes shot up toward the scoreboard. All tied up at 9 to 9. And the try for the extra point coming up. . . .

But even then, even while he was thinking ahead to the try for extra point, his thoughts went back to his freshman year; to baseball; to the left-handed throw he had made from right field in the Southeastern game. He had been hit on the right arm by a pitched ball and couldn't use it. The Southeastern base runner had counted on his bad right arm then . . . just as Western had today!

Red was being mobbed by Biggie and Brennan and Montague and then Speed came hobbling in to hold the ball. They huddled and then formed on the line and Chip's boot carried the ball high and true, between and far beyond the uprights, a perfect kick. The score: State 10, Western 9.

Chip and Red trotted back up the field together, pounding one another in sheer exultation, oblivious to the thundering tribute of the fans. And the tumult of the crowd was still booming down at them as Chip and his teammates lined up for the kick. Chip glanced up at the clock. A minute and fifty seconds left to play. . . .

He put all his might into the thrust of his leg and the ball soared high in the air and lit deep in the Western end zone, out of play. Western's ball on their own twenty-yard line, first and ten.

The Western players were panic-stricken, hurried the play, and someone missed his assignment. Biggie and Brennan crashed through the line and tackled the passer so viciously that he fumbled the ball. Soapy was right behind Biggie and Brennan and fell on the ball on the Western seventeen-yard line.

State's ball!

Chip watched the clock and used every possible second in the huddle and on the play. He took the ball from Brennan three straight times and dropped down to cover it with his arms and legs and body right where he stood. Then the crack of the gun ended the game and the gang lifted him up on their shoulders, and when he looked up at the scoreboard, it showed: State 10, Western 9.

Sunday afternoon Curly Ralston and his assistants worked feverishly in the head coach's office, discussing the strategy and the new attack he had devised expressly for the A. & M. game.

"We can call it the Convalescent Ward Offense," Bill Sullivan said pointedly. "Goodness knows we've got enough players on the injury list."

"What about Whittemore and the touchdown twins?" Rockwell asked. His question was directed toward no one in particular, but he was hoping Ralston would make some comment. But the head coach ignored it completely, and continued his study of the paper spread out on the table.

A little later Ralston nodded in satisfaction. "Well, see you the first thing in the morning."

Rockwell, Sullivan, and Nelson remained in the office after Ralston's departure and continued to discuss the new formation. Then the talk shifted to Whittemore and Aker and Jacobs. "I think he should give them a chance," Rockwell said.

"I agree," Nelson said.

"Well," Sullivan drawled, "much as I dislike the touchdown twins, I'll have to go along with that. We know Whittemore would help and Aker and Jacobs just *might*—note that I said might—help. It's worth a try."

"Tell that to the coach," Nelson said, smiling.

"You tell him!" Sullivan retorted.

"Well," Rockwell said, pulling on his coat, "I'm going home. We've got a tough week ahead."

The next afternoon and on Tuesday and Wednesday, Ralston spent half an hour with Chip and Young reviewing the new formation and the strategy plans for the game. And every day on the field and on the campus, the tension mounted. This was the *big* game of the season and of the year; not only because it meant the conference championship, but because of the intense football rivalry which had gripped the two schools for forty-nine straight years.

The game meant much to the regulars, but it was vital to the reserves; to play in one quarter of this traditional game cut in half the varsity letter requirements.

Friday night every available room in University was filled. And still the fans came, jamming the stores and streets and restaurants. It was a big business night for the local merchants and State Drug was no exception. Chip had hoped to see Skip play in the state championship game that night in the State Stadium but State Drug was mobbed. He and Soapy, Whitty, Fireball, and the rest of the staff had to settle for Gee-Gee Gray's radio account of the game.

Skip made a name for himself that night. It was his last high school game and the fans really gave him a send-off. Skip justified their faith, played one of the greatest games of his career, won the game almost singlehanded by his running, kicking, and passing.

After the game, the Tech High victory march started in the stadium and ended up in the business section of University adding to the confusion and football hysteria which gripped the city. Skip appeared at State Drug just before ten o'clock and George Grayson's employees took up where his personal fans had left off. It all added up to a tension-packed preliminary for the big show which was on tap for the next afternoon.

Mitzi Savrill had arranged for a taxi to be at the side door of the store at ten thirty. Chip, Soapy, Fireball, and Whitty piled in, anxious to get away from the hilarious fans and back to Jeff.

Chip had trouble going to sleep. Tomorrow's game would be the biggest game of his life; the first college championship game he had played as captain of a team and one which would have a big bearing on his standing as an All-America player. He was planning ahead for the next day, thinking about the game and his arm and the touchdown twins and Ralston and A. & M., for hours, it seemed, before, at last, he fell asleep.

CHAPTER 21

END-ZONE DISASTER

EVERY SEAT in the stadium was filled and the massive
array of colors—red, orange, yellow, blue, green, and
every imaginary blend which garbed the gay, festive
multitude—rivaled the beauty of the fleecy white
clouds up above in the clear blue sky. Chip and Fireball took turns booting the ball to Gary Young, Eddie
Aker, and Jack Jacobs. Fireball drilled one of his low,
cannon-ball spirals and Chip watched as Aker yelled
for the ball and pulled it in on the dead run.

That was the way Aker and Jacobs had put out all
week. They had worked at top speed during every
minute of the practices and had shown tremendous
snap and drive when running through the plays. Following the Western game, Chip had feared that they
might lapse back into their shells. But the touchdown
twins had given no indication that they had resented
sitting the bench.

A. & M. won the toss and elected to receive. Chip
chose to defend the north goal so the Statesmen
would have the wind at their backs and his kick carried into the end zone and out of bounds. A. & M.
took over on their own twenty-yard line, first and ten.

State's forward line, battling as it had all season, held the visitors to four scant yards in three downs. After several punt exchanges, Chip managed to break away and sprint to the Aggie's thirty. Three plays later, with the ball resting on the A. & M. twenty-three-yard line, Speed limped in to hold the ball and Chip kicked a perfect placement for the first score of the game.

The State fans went wild. But it was the last time they had cause to rejoice during the first half. Thereafter, the Statesmen could do nothing right and the Farmers nothing wrong. It might have been a different story if Speed and Ace had been in the game and in shape. As it was, Ralston shuffled his makeshift backfield time and again but to no avail.

Chip managed to break away a little later and Rockwell elbowed Ralston. "Look to the right," he said. "Look at Whittemore, Aker, and Jacobs."

The three prodigals were out on the edge of the field yelling for all they were worth, side by side with the rest of the reserves, rooting for Chip and their weary teammates. But, to the disappointment of Rockwell, the head coach turned back to the field, apparently indifferent to the trio.

A. & M.'s candidate for All-America honors, a mercurial halfback named Kerwin, was breaking the game wide open. Alternating at end and as a flanker back, he had Anderson and Horton bewildered; cutting past them, reversing, buttonhooking, and using all kinds of pass-receiving maneuvers to snare passes in their zones. He tallied twice in the first quarter and again just before the end of the second period.

The score at the half: A. & M. 19, State 3.

Between the halves, Murph Kelly sponged Chip's face and tested the shock cast. "All right?" he asked.

Chip nodded. "Sure, Murph. Fine."

"You don't *look* fine."

Murph was dead right. He wasn't fine by a long shot. The Aggies had given him a rough time, tackling him viciously and dumping him hard every time he carried the ball. There was nothing dirty about their play but they were giving him no quarter, bad shoulder notwithstanding.

His muscles were fighting back every command, aching and protesting and sluggishly obeying his will. He looked at his teammates. They were tired, too. Like himself, Soapy, Biggie, Fireball, Red, Brennan, O'Malley, Maxim, and Montague had played practically every minute through nine straight games. But they had never faltered and they had never quit. That was what football was all about, he reflected. A fellow gave all he had and then forced himself to give a little more. He fought for the team and his school and the coach and the game, loving the feeling that he was doing his best.

Ralston moved from player to player, patting a shoulder here and there and saying a few words to each of them. But his manner and bearing made words unnecessary. Chip and every player in the room knew that every fiber of the hard-working coach's being was with them all the way. He could give it and he could take it. *This was a man. . . .*

In the third quarter it started all over again. State received and the ball came spinning end over end all the way back to the goal line where Chip waited. It was a good kick and the confident Aggies came speeding toward him. The blocking was good up front; Soapy, Biggie, Red, Brennan, Maxim, and O'Malley each dumped a man. But the others couldn't handle the fast-moving ends and backs, and Chip went down under three of the eager tacklers on the twenty.

State couldn't advance the ball and Chip kicked. Now, for the first time, the Aggie attack stalled. But State couldn't take advantage of the opportunity. Chip tried Fireball as a passer but the A. & M. defense shifted just right every time; just as if their own quarterback had called the play. When Chip carried, he got clobbered. Only his superb kicking held A. & M. in check.

Early in the fourth quarter State had the ball on their own twenty-yard line, third and seven. Chip tried a reverse keeper and nearly got away with it. But Young's fake wasn't good enough and the Farmer right halfback caught him on the State thirty-eight-yard line. He made a shoestring tackle and Chip went down hard. Too hard.

Ralston sent Ken Knight in to replace Chip and Junior Roberts for Finley. Then he walked over and sat down on the bench beside Chip. "Are you all right?" he asked.

"I'm fine, Coach. They just knocked the wind out of me. I'm all right now."

Ralston shook his head in relief. "I'm glad to hear that. Now, this game isn't over. We've pulled out of worse spots."

"We can do it, Coach," Chip said. He leaned forward and gestured toward the end of the bench. "Couldn't you give Whittemore and Aker and Jacobs a chance, now? They're ready, Coach."

Ralston studied Chip's anxious face a moment. "All right, Hilton," he said. "You win!" He patted Finley on the shoulder. "All right, Finley?"

"Never better, Coach!"

Ralston nodded and turned toward the end of the bench where Whittemore, Aker, and Jacobs were sitting. "Whittemore!" he bellowed. "Aker! Jacobs! Here! On the double."

The three players nearly knocked one another over trying to be the first to reach Ralston. They pulled on their helmets and ringed Ralston, Chip, and Finley while the coach gave them their instructions. When the referee's whistle killed the ball on the next play, he sent all four in as a backfield unit.

It was third down, ten yards to go, with the ball on their own thirty-eight-yard line when Chip and his new backfield joined the linemen in the huddle. "We'll pass," he said, ignoring the relieved comments of the veterans. "Reverse 9 X! You're throwing, Eddie! On three, gang! Let's go!"

It worked! Aker's thirty-yard peg hit Whittemore on the Farmers' thirty-second-yard line and the big end made it to the Aggie twenty-five before he was downed.

The momentum of the game had shifted, now, and the State backfield became a symphony of action. With Chip handling the ball, Fireball plunging, and Aker and Jacobs alternating on tackle slants, the Statesmen scored in six plays. That made the score 19 to 9 and Chip decided to go for the two-point play.

"We'll run it!" he said decisively, grinning at the eager faces in the huddle. "Thirty-nine! That's you, Jack! On three! Let's go!"

He faked to Fireball and flipped the ball to Jacobs. The determined sophomore hit the line like a streak and smashed through for the two points. The score: A. & M. 19, State 11.

A. & M. received and Chip's kick carried to the goal line. This time, the ball carrier made it only to the twelve-yard line before he was dumped by Whittemore and Maxim. The Farmers suddenly realized they were up against a new team, a team which was back in the ball game, suddenly come alive, on fire, determined to win.

The Aggies fought to advance the ball but the State defenders were fighting like madmen and wouldn't give an inch. The Aggie kicker punted to Chip on the mid-field stripe and Chip cut wide to the right. Just as he was about to be tackled, he lateraled to Aker. But the ball slipped through Aker's hands and A. & M. recovered on their own forty-five-yard line.

Aker was upset and disgusted when he joined the defensive huddle. "My fault," he said remorsefully. "I was away clear. It would have been a touchdown."

"Forget it, Eddie," Brennan rasped. "We'll get it back."

Chip looked at the clock. Four minutes to play. . . .

The Aggies moved to the State fifteen-yard line before they could be stopped. Then, on fourth down, the quarterback attempted a pass which Chip knocked down with his left hand in the end zone. It was the Statesmen's ball on their own twenty, first and ten.

He called the play in the huddle, and when time was in, Aker hit Whittemore with a bullet pass just over the line. The big wing man threw off three tacklers before he was brought down on the forty-eight-yard line. Forty seconds to play. . . .

Chip faked to Fireball and went wide to the right on a keeper. Twisting and squirming, he made it to the A. & M. thirty-yard line. As soon as he was downed he yelled for a time-out. "Time!" he cried. "Time!"

Ten seconds left to play! Time for one more play. . . .

When time was in he gave the ball to Jacobs on a

fake dive play. Jacobs reversed and passed the ball to Whittemore just as the tall end crossed the Farmers' five-yard line. Whitty went far up above the defensive opponent and pulled in the ball for the touchdown. That made the score: A. & M. 19, State 17.

Everyone in the Stadium knew the play. State had to go for the two points and the tie. Two points to tie the score and to tie A. & M. for the conference championship.

A. & M. went into a close 5–3–3 defense as the Statesmen formed in the huddle. Chip called for a fake-pass play with Aker carrying over left tackle. "Make a hole—Biggie, Whitty!"

"We'll make it!" Biggie said grimly.

"On one, gang!" Chip said. "Let's go!"

Chip faked to Fireball and handed-off to Aker. Aker faked the pass to Whittemore and slanted for the hole Biggie and Whitty had made, a hole big enough to drive a wagon through. Then, a yard from the goal line, he fumbled!

The ball rolled across the goal line and Aker dove frantically after it, arms outstretched. Just as his hands reached the ball, the Aggie line-backer kicked it away and out of bounds.

Pandemonium reigned as the referee awarded a one-point safety to State. The players, coaches, spectators, and some of the officials had never heard of a one-point safety and many of the State supporters were still on the field and in the stadium arguing the point an hour after the referee had proved he was correct. It was right in the rule book and he showed it to Ralston, Rockwell, and Chip.

The final score: A. & M 19, State 18.

There went the season and the conference title and all they had fought for through nine disaster-loaded games. All for the sake of one little point. Just like that. . . .

Chip and Ralston and Rockwell managed to edge through the hysterical crowd of Aggie fans and into the A. & M. dressing room long enough to congratulate the visitors' coach and captain. Then they walked slowly along the aisle to the Statesmen's quarters. Pausing just inside the door they surveyed the scene. Aker and Jacobs were surrounded by every State player in the room.

"But I lost the game!" Aker was saying. "I ruined the season! Everything!"

"Nuts!" Biggie shouted, clamping his big arms around the touchdown twins. "*We* lost the game. The *team* lost the game!"

"Yeah!" Red shouted. "But wait until next year! We'll all be back!"

"Right!" Soapy yelled. "Come New Year's next year we'll be eating strawberries in the Rose Bowl!"

CHAPTER 22

THE COVETED TROPHY

THE SPEAKERS' TABLE at the front of the big banquet hall extended clear across the room and every place was occupied by a notable from the football world. Chip, seated at the head of the Statesmen's table, turned to check the persons at the speakers' table with the names listed on his program. E. Merton Blaine was sitting in the toastmaster's chair, with Coach Ralston on his right and Coach Carpenter on his left.

A man with all the earmarks of an athlete was seated beside Ralston and the program listed him as Stew Peterson, Brand University. Chip studied the famous coach. His tanned face indicated an outdoor life and his broad, compact body spelled football. *So this was the famous coach who was going to guide Skip's future in football.* . . .

Henry Rockwell, Nibs Nelson, and Jim Sullivan were seated at the right end of the table and several other men who Chip figured were Tech High administrators and coaches were seated at the left. In between, he noted Bill Bell, sports editor of the *Herald*, Gee-Gee Gray, sports broadcaster, and Jim Locke, of the *News*.

The members of the Tech team were seated at a

long table on the right side of the speakers' table and the State players were seated with Chip on the left. Skip sat directly opposite him at the head of the Tech table and Chip caught his eye. Skip's face was glum, but it brightened briefly as he acknowledged Chip's smile. Then the smile disappeared and he began to study his program.

After the invocation came the food. And it kept coming! Hors d'oeuvres; shrimp cocktails; soups and salads; roast turkey and cranberry sauce; big, thick steaks; mashed potatoes with gravy; peas and all sorts of fresh vegetables; and then came peach melba, pie and ice cream, milk, tea, and coffee.

Later, while the bus boys were clearing the tables, the orchestra played the Tech football march and the Tech players sang the words. Then they played the Tech alma mater and everyone stood up and listened to the beautiful words and music of the song. Then everyone sat down and E. Merton Blaine welcomed the guests and the program got under way.

Chip was thinking about Skip and Mr. Blaine, although he heard most of what the speakers had to say. There wasn't any question about the purpose of Stew Peterson's presence. A big-time coach like Peterson didn't come clear across the country just to attend a high school banquet.

Coach Ralston was introduced and Chip gave him all of his attention. This was *his* coach. Chip was listening to him and wishing that all the youngsters in the country could have coaches like Curly Ralston and Henry Rockwell. They were two of a kind; keen, alert students of the game; inspiring leaders and understanding teachers with a strict moral code which brooked no equivocation.

Just as Chip expected, Ralston gave the credit to

the team and its fighting spirit for the victories and he had no alibis for the defeats. And like the great coach he was, he said he was looking forward to "next year!"

At the end, Ralston praised Tech's great team and paid special tribute to Skip Miller. When he finished, Chip was one of the first to get to his feet and applaud State's great football leader.

Mr. Blaine was standing, now, waiting for the applause to end. But the people assembled there, and especially Chip and his teammates, weren't going to leave the slightest vestige of doubt in anyone's mind just how they felt about Ralston. Finally the applause died away and Mr. Blaine began to speak.

"I've listened to a lot of speeches in my time," Blaine said, "but that was one of the greatest. And by one of the finest gentlemen it has ever been my privilege to meet.

"Now, we come to the first of the awards scheduled on this program. As you know, this dinner was given in honor of Tech High School's state championship team. And we will get to that in a few minutes.

"At the beginning of this program I introduced Coach Stew Peterson of Brand University. Now, he has a message of importance to every football fan in the country. Stew—"

Coach Peterson smiled and acknowledged the flurry of applause. Lifting a hand, he waited until there was absolute silence. "My part in this wonderful affair is of extreme importance to my colleagues who are members of the National Collegiate Football Coaches Association.

"Each year, as most of you are aware, the Association makes certain awards. This year, it is my honor to be chairman of the awards committee. So I speak to you as an official representative of all of the college coaches in this country.

"Gentlemen, athletes, friends, it is my privilege to confer a trophy and announce—for the second consecutive year—the selection of the current year's All-America quarterback—Chip Hilton!"

The roar which filled the banquet hall lifted Chip right out of his chair with the others. His teammates pushed him forward and lifted him on their shoulders in front of Stew Peterson. They were yelling and Peterson was pumping his hand.

Coach Peterson pressed the All-America trophy into his hands and his teammates put him down. Then Skip had him by the hand and Aker and Jacobs had their arms around his shoulders and the lump in his throat was as big as a football and he couldn't say a word.

To be an All-America player was a great thing. But it wasn't the biggest thing in football. The biggest thing was to be a part of the team, to be one of those who stood side by side and fought for one another in a common cause which was clean and good; where the greatest reward was the priceless feeling of knowing you had given your best for your friends and the thing you were fighting for. . . .

It was five minutes before the audience quieted. Chip found himself back at the State table clutching the coveted trophy in his hands, a thousand thoughts whirling through his mind; his mother, Soapy, Biggie, Speed, Rockwell, Red, Fireball, Whitty, Skip, Ralston, Aker, Jacobs, Peterson, Blaine. . . .

Coach Carpenter was presenting trophies to his players, now, and Chip joined in the applause for them. Skip was the last to receive a trophy and the ovation was deafening. When it quieted, Coach Carpenter was so affected that he couldn't say a word; he stood there speechless, clasping Skip's hand.

Mr. Blaine came to Carpenter's rescue. "I have come to know Coach Bill Carpenter this past football season almost as well as I know my nephew—Skip Miller. Bill is a great leader and friend of youth, a man devoted to his chosen profession and to the youngsters he coaches. *I* know what he wanted to say to Skip and I am sure *you* know.

"Skip has captained and led two of Coach Carpenter's teams to state championships. At the same time, he has won great honors for himself. As you know, he has been selected as All-State quarterback for two straight years. And that brings me to an important announcement."

There was a dead silence. Chip and every person in the room knew what this was all about. . . .

"Skip has been imitating Chip Hilton for two years; his quarterbacking and his kicking and running and passing—even his crew cuts.

"And I want Skip Miller to *keep on* imitating Chip Hilton. So much so that when Skip is a sophomore, ready to play college football, he'll be ready to take Chip Hilton's place—"

Blaine paused and turned to smile down at Stew Peterson and then continued, "And when Brand University meets State in the Rose Bowl, Skip Miller will be calling the plays for his home-town team, for the school representing the state in which he was born."

A little buzz began in the back of the room and grew and grew until it burst into a deafening shout of surprise and jubilation just after Blaine lifted his glass of water in a toast and cried:

"Here's to Chip Hilton and to State's next All-America quarterback—Skip Miller!"

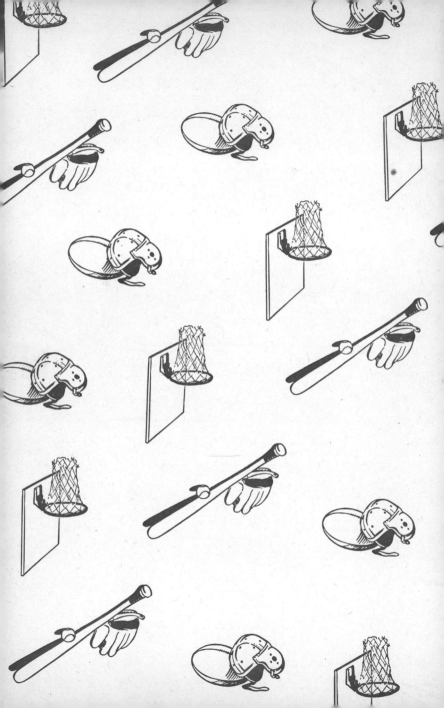